TASTING HIM

TASTING HIM

ORAL SEX STORIES

EDITED BY
RACHEL KRAMER BUSSEL

CLEIS
PRESS

Cleis Press Inc., P.O. Box 14697, San Francisco, California 94114
Printed in the United States.

Cover design: Scott Idleman
Cover photograph: April/Getty Images
Text design: Frank Wiedemann
Cleis logo art: Juana Alicia
First Edition.
10 9 8 7 6 5 4 3 2 1

Contents

INTRODUCTION: THE POWER AND PLEASURE OF COCKSUCKING

It's common knowledge that I have a decided oral fixation, and to me, nothing signals the culmination of that fixation better than giving a blow job. In so many ways, it's my favorite erotic act in and of itself, or as foreplay. Sometimes, our culture sends the message that those who enjoy going down are somehow only doing the bidding of someone else who's getting all the pleasure. Caitlin Flanagan asked in *The Atlantic Monthly* in a rambling review of the young adult novel *Rainbow Party*, "Whatever happened to the hand job? Whither the dry hump? Why do girls prefer the far more debasing, uncomfortable, and messy blow job?" What she doesn't realize is that some of us enjoy blow jobs precisely because they can be "debasing, uncomfortable, and messy." We like to savor those sensations, engage with the power play, get off on being "ordered" to do it. Or we lustily get down on our knees and demand that our lovers give us their cocks. We know that the power of a good blow job goes both ways, and now, we want you to know just how hot it makes us.

What's special about *Tasting Him,* though, is that these aren't your usual blow jobs. There's no rush to get the "job" aspect of it over with. There's power play in these blow jobs and, just to be clear, they're not all "hims" receiving them. Oh, no. Here, cocks are real and metaphorical, made of solid flesh and even more solid silicone. Here, men and women get down on their knees and take what's rightfully theirs. Women discover the power of getting a blow job, while a few men surprise themselves with their own prowess.

Recently, I read an amazing story, "Me, When I'm with You," by Matthilde Madden, in my friend Alison Tyler's anthology *H Is for Hardcore.* In it, a woman gives a man a blow job. Nothing that unusual there…except that she's the top in the story, a woman who rules the roost, who orders her lover to spend whole days naked. She reigns over him, and yet she manages to go down on him without losing control. She reclaims the act of taking a man's member into her mouth, showing him who's really in charge. Madden wrote, "I love sucking your cock. It took me a while to find a suitably dom way of sucking your cock, but eventually I discovered that if your hands were tied behind your back and your ankles were forced apart with a spreader bar and your nipples were clamped and I had a vibrator tight against your arsehole, that worked for me."

That is precisely the kind of energy I wanted to bring to this book. There are blow-job queens and blow-job virgins, those who are squeamish and those who are shy. There are those who live to suck cock and those who live to get their cocks sucked. There are lessons of the practical and more ephemeral to be learned here.

While I can't guarantee that this book will lead to better blow jobs (though I do encourage you, like the protagonist in Scarlett French's "Fellatio: A Love Story," to check out Violet Blue's how-to book *The Ultimate Guide to Fellatio*), I can strongly predict that you won't be able to make it all the way through these twenty-three tales without having to put your hands down your pants. Whether you possess one or not, you'll likely want to get your dick sucked by the end of this book, unless your mouth is too busy watering.

Like French's character, there are many teachers and students here, some eager to learn all they can about how to make the experience hotter and juicier for their lovers, and some who are shown the ropes by those who care enough to explain exactly what gets them off. In stories like Robert Peregrine's "A Treatise on Human Nature," a man tries to teach his new female lover "how to give head like a man," while in "Quite a Mouthful: Confessions of a Sweet Cocksucker" by Tish Andersen and "Without Eyes" by Terri Pray, the kinky women in these stories get over their fears and let their masters take control of their mouths, then thrill to the slurping sounds and sensations of real submission. And "Tony Tempo," the title character in Tsaurah Litzky's story, shows you're never too old to enjoy a perfectly pursed pair of lips.

Another natural theme here involves oral pleasure of a different sort. Food and fellatio seem to go, well, hand in mouth, as seen in Alison Tyler's inventive "Prego," involving, yes, the spaghetti sauce, Kristina Wright's cinnamon roll treat "Frosted," and Donna George Storey's exploration of the famed powers of an "After Dinner Mint," or in this case, liqueur, on a blow job. All speak to the sensual power of a hungry mouth, and show the ways both appetites can be satisfied at the same time.

The getter and giver are both worshipped in these stories. While many tell of an insatiable yearning for a full mouth, others share the thrill, both corporeal and visual, of the blow job, along with the pronounced power dynamics. In "Blessed Benediction," prolific erotica writer Radclyffe gives us some insight into what it's like to watch the one you love put her pretty little lips to good use:

Now, the reason my girl is such a great cocksucker is that she understands that a blow job is as much about the show as it is about her hot, wet mouth sliding up and down my cock until I come in her mouth. She doesn't go down on me like it's a chore, or penance, or a favor. She turns giving head into a work of art. Every move is designed to let me know she gets off on my cock, and that teasing my rod makes her cream.

Hers and other stories here show that you don't have to be a man to have a cock, or to enjoy having it licked, sucked, and swallowed. Getting a blow job is about both the physical sensation, and the view, whether she's blindfolded as in Pray's story, or staring up at you while her (or his) mouth is full.

Tasting Him pays tribute to those who enjoy the act, and art, of fellatio wherever it occurs—in a bed, in the crashing surf, as in Alessia Brio's "Down on the Beach," or at a kitchen table, as in Tenille Brown's "Getting Used to It." I hope it turns you on as much to read these tales as it did me to edit them.

Rachel Kramer Bussel
New York City

GLOSS

Rachel Kramer Bussel

Standing in front of the mirror, I apply the gooey liquid to my lips until they shine like glass, not gooey but slick and hard, almost icy. I'm keeping in mind my friend Alice's advice that "lip gloss should look like you've just given someone a blow job." Whether or not they fulfill this maxim, I know my lips will be the main attraction tonight, which is precisely the idea. They are slick and shiny, like a red race car, boldly drawing attention to themselves, whether the viewer wants to look or not. The rest of my ensemble works, too, clingy black top and short, tight black PVC skirt. But I want people's eyes firmly on my lips.

I head over to the bar, a plush new one that's just opened. I've been lucky enough to land a coveted invitation to this private party, and I know the crowd will be the cream of the crop. I could have brought a guest, but tonight is by necessity a solo excursion. I'm on a specific mission and need to conduct it in my own way. Finding the right man for a one-night stand, for an electric connection that burns and sizzles as fast and hot as a firecracker, and lasts about as long, requires a unique combination of savvy and intuition, and I can't have any distractions.

Red is the theme of the night, with lush red curtains and a deep garnet shade painted on the walls. I order the watermelon martini, the night's special, and perch on the bar stool. My legs are tucked under the bar and I don't bother to showcase them, even though I know they're magnificent. I'm alone and know exactly what I want: a hot guy, a stud, someone to entertain me for tonight and tonight only. Someone with a cock that's hard and hot and needy, just for me. As I close my eyes and lean forward to sip the cold, sweet drink, I feel a presence behind me. After I swallow, I slowly sit up in my chair, leaning back ever so slightly and brushing against the shirtfront of a very slick, well-dressed, handsome man. Not a cute, shaggy hipster like I normally meet or a yuppie Wall Streeter straight out of college, but a real man—a little older, crisp and clean, sophisticated.

I slowly swivel my stool around to look at him, our gazes holding. My knees skim his thighs, and instead of smiling, I reach for my glass and bring it to his lips. The ghost of a smile forms on his face as he lets me tilt the icy red liquid down his throat. I bring the glass back to my own lips and sip again, slowly and deliberately, still meeting his gaze. I'm vaguely aware of the crowd surging around us, the commotion at the bar, but this stranger is occupying the bulk of my attention. I have the urge to wrap my legs around his waist and draw him closer, but I stay composed. I open my mouth, searching for a witty line to introduce myself, but the longer we stare at each other, the more difficult words become.

Instead, I take his left hand and bring it to my mouth, sliding his index finger inside and then carefully sliding it out, my tongue pressing against it the entire time. I push it back in again and repeat the process, this time lightly grazing my teeth along his slightly roughened skin. As I'm about to go for a third round, he moves his hand and trails his wet finger along my neck, ending at the neckline of my dress, his hand resting on my chest.

He reaches his hand out for mine and even though I have half a drink left, I let him lead me into the unisex single-occupancy bathroom. As befits the rest of the décor, the bathroom is lush and lavish, with red tiles and smooth surfaces and a sumptuous upholstered chair along with the sink and toilet. I look up at him, my lips slightly pursed, poised to smile or laugh or smirk, not letting him know which one it will be yet. I keep my eyes locked on his as my hand goes to his crotch, feeling the heat and hardness beneath. I like that I'm in control here, that even though I just met him, I know that he's at my mercy. He led me here but now I will be leading him. Even down on my knees, I will be the one in control and that thought sends a shiver through my body. Ignoring the chair for a moment, I step closer and then drag myself down his body, my breasts sliding along his torso, my nipples hardening at the friction as I sink to the floor. It's hard to keep my commanding gaze as I look up at him, but somehow I manage even though inside I'm melting. I close my eyes for a second as my hand reaches up reverently to stroke his cock through his pants.

I glance briefly at the chair but then realize that I like it better down here on the cold floor, the tiles pressing into my knees as I fumble with his belt buckle. I'm soaking wet and will surely have to remove my panties later, but for the moment all I care about is his cock and getting it into my mouth. He helps me undo his zipper and before his pants are even pushed down his thighs, I'm leaning forward, my tongue darting forth to lick a slow, teasing line along the length of his cock. I move closer so my knees are pressed up against the sides of his shoes, my legs slightly spread as I try to taste all of him at once. He sighs and groans and I look up at him for a moment, no longer smirking at all, simply acknowledging how right it feels to be here in front of him. His eyes are almost too intense and I close mine before guiding the length of his smooth, warm cock into my mouth, going slowly until I have all of him inside of me.

I try to push him deeper, to feel the tip of his cock at the back of my throat, to take him as far inside of me as I can. I hold his cock and press the tip along my throat, ecstatic, until finally sliding it out and starting the whole process all over again. I tilt my head and run my pursed lips along his cock, up and down and around, making it my own slippery sexual harmonica that I can play any way I want. I love the way he feels against me, how hot his cock is, and every time I move to try something else like licking his balls or kissing my way along his length, I suddenly need to have him inside me again. I devour his cock, slamming it down my throat and back, rocking my whole body back and forth in a special kind of dance. As I do, my thong presses tightly against my pussy, and I let out a groan of my own that reverberates against his cock. I feel like I could stay right here forever, learn every curve and crevice and nuance of his cock, and still want more.

He is enjoying it too, I can tell, but as his hands flick agitatedly from my head to my hair to his sides, I know he's getting close and I don't want to deprive him. I slide him slowly out of my mouth, teasing him by sliding his dick back in slightly and then continuing. I rub my cheeks against his cock, then press his hardness against my neck, caress it and adore it. Then I spread my legs wider, into a split, and look up at him before opening my mouth, sticking out my tongue and slapping his cock against it again and again. Now he really groans, louder and fiercer than before, and I move faster, then shake my head back and forth, slapping my face against his cock and his cock against my face in a frenzy that makes me feel almost dizzy. I want to talk, to tell him to please come for me, to tell him how much I need his hot come splattered all over me, to tell him how wet he's making me, but I don't want to ruin the mood. I think he knows how I feel, though, as we thrash energetically, and then he grabs my head with one hand and his cock with the other and forces his come onto me, giving me exactly what I'd silently asked for as the warm whiteness spills all over my face, my lips, my hair. I lunge for his cock and suck the rest of it out of him, holding him there even after I know he's done.

Finally I stand up, too nervous to look at him. Instead I look in the mirror and try to rearrange my hair and clothes so that it's not quite so obvious what we've been doing. It feels like we've been here for an hour but I think it's only been about ten minutes, which is still long enough to annoy the bar patrons. I smooth my hair back into its barrettes, adjust my dress, splash water on my cheeks and wipe them clean. But my lips, well, my lips I leave, looking wet and moist and red and sexy. I don't need the lip gloss anymore to do the job for me; I've just done it myself. I wink at the stranger and then stroll out the door, a smile on my wet red lips.

A TREATISE ON HUMAN NATURE

Robert Peregrine

I want to learn to give head like a man," she said. "Tell me how it's different." In a drunken moment of openness, I had told her about my bisexual past, a youthful experiment that I was growing out of in my early thirties. Usually, when I was trying to pick up women in bars, I kept this information to myself. A lot of women were turned off by a man who'd had sex with other men, but then, once in a while, the truth crept out, and luckily, this particular woman—Tracie was her name—was intrigued, wanted to know all about it, was obviously turned on by the very idea. I supposed that one of the reasons my secret had slipped out was because we were getting along so well, and my guard was down. We were both singing along animatedly when an old song by The Smiths came on the jukebox, and the topic of conversation had very casually taken a turn from the singer Morrissey's alleged asexuality to sexual orientation in general.

When I'd admitted to having had bisexual experiences, she

asked me whether men or women gave better blow jobs, and I said—because it's generally true—that beyond a doubt, men do. A man knows what it feels like to receive a blow job, and so it's obvious that a man would have a better instinct about how to give one. It was clear to me that this got Tracie's feminist dander up. She was very competitive, she said, and thought she should be able to learn to do this as well as any man could, despite the drawback of not having a penis of her own. Besides that, she'd been told by men that she was very good at it, but as far as she knew, none of those men had ever gotten head from another man. So the challenge was on, and I took her back to my apartment to discuss it further.

It was a short walk from the Greenwich Village bar to my place in Chelsea. We laughed and flirted all the way up 7th Avenue, talking about our lives, getting to know one another. She was a copy editor, and I was a techie doing various types of freelance computer work, from programming to web design. She was a native New Yorker, and I was originally from Alabama. Her father was South American, which explained the slightly ambiguous ethnicity that I found exotic and interesting about her. Along the way, we made fun of people we saw who were dressed poorly or acting bizarre, such as one typically sees on a Friday night in Manhattan. A casual observer would have thought we were old pals, would never have guessed that we just met an hour before in a bar. When I opened the door to my apartment, though, I immediately came back to the reason we were here—a lesson in giving a blow job like a man.

"First of all," I told her as I flicked on the lights, "you have to really want it, and not like you want a piece of candy. It's not a lollipop. You have to want it like you want a piece of steak. You have to be ravenous for it. Typically, women suck cock. Men devour it."

"An interesting distinction," she said. "But no teeth, of course?"

"Absolutely. You do have to keep your teeth out of the way. That goes without saying. I'm talking more about the attitude, the mental state. We'll get around to what you actually do with your mouth, but if you can't get into a man's mind, none of that will matter."

I offered her a seat on the couch and then went into my bedroom to retrieve a dildo, letting her think over what I'd told her. When I returned, I said, "Now we'll get to that other part."

Sitting down next to her on the sofa, I took the dildo into my mouth to demonstrate for her what I meant, and I could feel my eyes rolling back as I hungrily deep-throated the silicone cock, thinking about the last time a real cock had been there, a couple of years before—a college student named Anthony I'd met on the Internet and made a date with when I'd only been in New York a few weeks. Anthony had been slim and muscular, a little taller than me. He was an Italian American from Queens, though not as hairy as many men who shared his heritage, and his olive skin contrasted nicely with my Anglo ivory. His cock also had been slender and long, like his body as a whole. After a minute or two, I remembered that I was supposed to be playing instructor, so I pointed out that I always kept my index finger and thumb around the shaft, and I showed her how I moved it up and down steadily, kneading loose skin, which the dildo actually lacks, so she would have to imagine that part.

"I understand some of what you're saying, and I'm enjoying watching you too," she said. "But, you know, I can't see what's going on inside your mouth."

"That's true. Let me show you. Hold out two fingers." Her delicate fingers made for a relatively small cock, but it would do for my purposes. I let the slender, pale digits linger playfully under my nose for a moment. "Imagine that this part, from the knuckle up, is the head." I then went down on her fingers, and I could see that she was enjoying it immensely. Her eyes closed, and her body stiffened. I wondered what could be going on in her imagination.

After a couple of minutes, she collected herself. "I feel what your tongue is doing," she said. "You're putting pressure on the underside. It's like you're making out with it. That's cool. You use more pressure with your tongue as you get closer to the tip. That's a good trick."

I stopped for a second to confirm what she was saying. "That area just under the hood is the most sensitive part, as the women's magazines always tell you."

"Hey, how do you know that? You're secretly reading Cosmo?"

I laughed. "C'mon. I look at them when I'm waiting in line at the grocery store. I want to know what they're telling you about us. So, anyway, they're right when they tell you to pay special attention to that area, but what kind of attention?"

"Um, focused pressure with the tongue?"

I was getting a kick out of the clinical tone of our conversation. But I decided it was time to take the lesson to the next stage, and my cock was already rigid from the preliminary demonstrations. "Why don't you show me what you mean instead of telling me?" I said as I unzipped my pants.

She grinned and said okay. She bent down and put my entire cock in her mouth, lubricating the shaft with her saliva. Placing her fingers around the shaft, she started pumping it, leaving only the head between her lips, and she flicked at the area under the hood with her tongue. "You're just teasing it," I said. "Remember what I was doing with your fingers a few minutes ago."

She started to get it, though I had to tell her to apply more suction, and then I just sat back and enjoyed the fruits of my teaching. My mind began to wander again back to Anthony. Other than the sex, we'd had nothing whatsoever to talk about. I'd asked him about his interests, and he seemed not to have any. Still, that tight, muscular body of his was a thrill. He said he'd never been with a man before, so I'd been a teacher to him as well, if I could believe him. In any case, he must have had a good time because he wanted to see me again. I was flattered, but as much as I liked his body, it was too dull hanging out with him before and afterward. I guessed that was why I didn't really consider myself bisexual anymore. I could have fun with their body parts, but men just didn't make good companions as far as I was concerned.

Just then, Tracie surprised me by putting a finger in my ass. She'd get bonus points for that. I could feel myself about to explode, so I told her to pump harder and fuck my ass with that finger. Soon, my body was convulsing with orgasmic waves, my back arched, and my hips lurched forward. Tracie filled her mouth with the load and then fed it back to me with a deep kiss. I felt my own come sliding down my throat and her tongue pressed against mine.

When I'd recovered enough to speak, I said, "You get an A." Tracie laughed. "By the way," I continued. "You never mentioned if you've ever gotten head from a woman."

"Well," she blushed. "As a matter of fact..."

The lesson continued from there, through the remainder of the night, and continues to this day.

QUITE A MOUTHFUL: CONFESSIONS OF A SWEET COCKSUCKER

Tish Andersen

Standing in Babeland, my local sex toy store, surrounded by naughty books, whips, dildos, and vibrators of all shapes and sizes, I can't help but think about all the dirty fun we've had. Right here in the sex shop I am daydreaming. Fantasizing about the things you've taught me: the time you tied my hands above my head and jerked off on me while you made me watch, unable to touch, lick, or assist. Or when you first went down on me, the whiskers of your mustache tickling the insides of my thighs and making them twitch against the ropes that held them wide open. How you taught me to suck your cock until you came, letting every last drop fill my mouth. Oh, and the time you forced me to suck you off while you paddled me, spanking harder and rougher the closer you were to orgasm.

I always loved sucking cock, but disliked—and in a sense, dreaded—the climactic eruption. I'd always (subtly) directed guys to come on my tits, or on my belly, even offering up my wide soft ass as a target, anywhere but in my mouth. I'd had bad experiences growing up—the guy who shot it in my eye and laughed while it burned, the guy who failed to warn me when he was about to come and flooded my unsuspecting mouth and throat with salty hot shots of sperm. But I loved you, wanted to please you, and knew it was what you wanted. You wanted me to keep my lips and tongue on your cock as you came and afterward, while I milked you, you'd tell me how hot it made you, how good it felt.

I wanted to do it. I just had to get over my fear and the preconditioning of ten-plus years of oral-sex technique that relied heavily on my ability to dodge the release. I even practiced first, tasting your come off my belly as it warmed against my skin and ran in dribbles down my side. Ever the thoughtful gentleman, you had a fresh minitowel next to my side of the bed, ready for easy cleanup. You told me it might be different with you, that you'd had a vasectomy and that your ejaculate had no sperm in it. In general, you smelled and tasted good, and I loved to sniff and lick you. Maybe it would be different...perhaps it would be different with you.

I was so proud of myself the first time I did it! You kept warning me that you were about to come, but I kept right on sucking, slurping, and licking and you came in my mouth, my lips wrapped firmly around your penis's military helmet. I tongued the underside of your cockhead and watched you jump and quiver. When the aftershocks died down, I felt smug. Satisfied. Womanly. I knew I had done that to you. The satisfaction I felt then was almost as good as the orgasm I had on your fingers sometime later that night.

Your teachings were like a journey for me, traversing the hills and valleys of my own sexuality. Being forced to watch myself (you so handily had those triple mirrors set up) as I orgasmed over your knee—my freshly spanked and reddened bottom up in the air; my pussy lips purpling, engorged with blood, slick with moisture—taught me to recognize the signs of my impending climax. All the things you taught me, still locked up tight inside my head, caused my skin to glow and my body to bloom. My friends couldn't stop commenting on how good I looked. They didn't know our secrets, although they probably could have guessed by watching us closely.

When I think about us sexually, specific events sort of run together, forming a mélange of sex-filled nights (and mornings). I recall how I used to tremble and shake as you watched me, really watched me, over your glasses rim. Sometimes I felt like a bug under a microscope, pinned helpless before your incisive and questioning eyes.

I think about the night you tied me to my bed, wrists together and overhead, my legs wide apart at the corners of the bed. I couldn't have moved even if I'd wanted to. I could feel the chafing from the hastily purchased leather wrist and ankle restraints, smell the scent of the leather warming from my body. (Even now, when I smell leather I think of you, and flush.) Listening to you talk about all the filthy things you were going to do to me had me in a twist. You seemed to know that my brain was my most potent sex organ, and you used all that mental foreplay to your advantage. I gasped and whimpered as you whispered in my ear, filling my head with thoughts of blow jobs and spankings to come.

That night, though, you were going to teach me another lesson, or so you said. You straddled my chest, your cock huge in front of my widened eyes. Looking up at you, unable to move—your eyes inspecting mine, deciphering my emotions as they flickered across my face—I was nervous. What was it that you had planned for me? You started to stroke yourself, soft long strokes over your shaft, up to the head and over before starting the process anew. You told me how you were going to come on my face, coating me in your ejaculate, and how I'd like it. It's not degrading, you wanted me to learn; it's okay, you said. Watching your cock grow longer, harder, and feeling the drip of precome as it hit my chest, I wondered what it would feel like. Were you really going to leave me tied up and helpless while you came all over my face? Yes. That's exactly what you did. As you got more excited, your voice turned husky, and the fantasies you spoke of swirled around my thoughts, taking control of and hijacking my feelings. I could smell my own arousal drifting up toward my nose, and I was embarrassed to think you could as well. Whimpering, I tried to rub my legs together, desperate to get my clitoral-hood piercing to provide friction against my straining clit, to no avail. My legs were tied apart tightly, and the more I tugged and squirmed, the more I seemed to excite you.

"Who do you belong to?" you demanded.

"Whose are you?" you asked over and over again, until I broke and cried out: "Yours! I'm yours. I belong to you and only you." A dam seemed to break in both of us at that moment, a dissolving of barriers and a crashing down of defenses.

You were on the verge of orgasm, but as you got closer, my trepidation increased. I felt ashamed but excited, embarrassed yet aroused. It was hard to believe that was me, trussed up while a man I loved—and, somewhat, feared—was about to come all over my face. As you came, warm white spurts hit my face, my forehead, my hair, my cheeks, dribbling down over my chin onto my neck and chest. You stayed there, watching me closely for a long time as your release cooled on my body. You rubbed some into my chest with your fingers, holding them up to my lips to taste.

I have no idea how long we stayed that way. It took quite some time before you got up, wet a cloth with hot water, and gently cleaned me up. Holding my chin with your thick fingers, you wiped the drying come off me, telling me all along what a good girl I was. I was buzzed off the experience, high on an endorphin safari. Odd, as I was the submissive one, I again felt powerful, female, and desirable. I patiently waited as you finished cleaning and grooming me, then watched as you untied me and rubbed my wrists between your warm, rough hands, hands that were capable of inflicting pain and pleasure, sometimes simultaneously.

Lost in my thoughts and fantasies, I forget for the moment that I am still at Babeland. As the fog of arousal clears a bit and I look around the store, my eyes (and the rest of me) are naturally drawn to the BDSM section of the shop, which is filled with whips, crops, clamps, and paddles. I blush a bit remembering the way you combined my darkest and deepest thoughts into a fully fleshed-out fantasy starring the two of us. Well, the two of us and a cameo by Elvis, my curious fat cat, sitting at the edge of the bed and looking on in bemusement.

During a late-night phone chat I had breathlessly revealed my desire to taste you, to give you a blow job while you spanked me. The thought left me delirious with want, the idea so stimulating and taboo I almost couldn't share it. It was hard for me to even say the word *spanking* aloud, but you weren't satisfied until you'd plumbed the depth of my dreams, mining for the dark, the forbidden, the sexual magic that turned me to quivering jelly. Red faced and fairly humming with tension, I told you about my hunger for using my newfound oral skills to bring you to orgasm as you paddled my asscheeks faster and harder, urging me onward.

I wasn't sure how or when you would do it, but I knew you would. The mental mind-fuck of waiting was hard, as was staring you in the face when we next met, after such an admission. Knowing that you knew left me vulnerable, soft, and weak-kneed. Was my naughty dream safe with you? I'd soon know.

Over hot chocolate at the Pick Me Up Café, you quietly told me that when I finished my drink, you were going to take me home, tie my hands behind my back, and lay me facedown on the bed. You told me to think about what might happen next as I drank my now lukewarm chocolate and you left me to stew and fret. Should I gulp down my remaining beverage in an effort to get the inevitable over with or should I slowly sip the drink, stretching the time until there wasn't a drop left? I felt apprehensive but aroused, my mind reeling with possibilities. I could feel your gaze on me, your eyes watching me, reading the expressions that flickered across my features in rapid succession. You always said you could read me, that my face gave it all away. Cursing my fair skin and expressive nature, I drank the last bit of cocoa, and, somewhat regretfully, put the mug back on the saucer. You left the tip and took me by the wrist.

I barely remember the walk home. The crisp autumn air, the kids still playing ball in the dying light at Tompkins Square Park, the taste of the chocolate still on my tongue—nothing really registered. Once at home it was only a matter of time. I stood still as you stripped me. You bound my wrists behind my back, leaving some slack for good measure. I felt you check and recheck the Japanese silk ropes, ascertaining that there was plenty of room for circulation. You pulled me toward you and kissed me gently, before taking off your own clothes. I shivered at the sound of your belt coming loose from its restraining loops. Once we were both naked, you positioned me on the bed, several pillows under my hips and chest. My head in your lap, you held your cock to my lips. My mouth felt dry, but I managed to take the soft length of you between my lips, feeling you harden as I held you there.

I began to lick and suck you as best I could without the aid of my hands. I was deep into my own headspace, your hand wrapped firmly in my hair, the scent of you in my nostrils, the sounds I made as I sucked your stiffening cock loudly echoing in my ears, when I heard rather than felt the swishing of the paddle before it landed on my upturned ass. The resulting crack shocked me enough to lose my grip on you, and you fell from my lips. I struggled to pull you back in, gasping as the paddle hit my cheeks again and again. My bottom was warming as you and I developed a rhythm. Spank, suck, spank, suck…. I hoped I was pleasing and satisfying you, but it was hard to concentrate on the task at hand. Or rather, the task without hands.

As I began to moan against your rigid erection, the combined warmth from my flushed face and your heated thighs caused sweat to drip down my forehead. Sweat and drool pooled at the base of your cock and around your balls as I worked harder and harder, the paddle urging me on. Not only did I suck, but I licked and nibbled (gently), and used the flat of my tongue in broad swipes from base to mushroom head. Your hips began to thrust in the telltale sign of your approaching orgasm, so I did my best deep-throating, just the way you liked. Spanking me with increased determination, you shot into my mouth and down my throat as I pressed my pussy into the pillow now, wet with my own juices. As I was still swallowing everything you had to offer, you paddled me one last time with the shiny black and red leather paddle, then laid it at your side.

After you untied me, we curled up in my big blue bed, quiet and peaceful. I knew we'd talk about what happened, but I was relieved you weren't making me discuss it just yet. A fantasy fulfilled is a wondrous thing, and it takes time to process it all. Plus, your recent blow job, my sore bottom, your wandering and caressing hand, and my pent-up lust caused more pressing things to come to mind. My orgasm that night caused my toes to curl and the obligatory fireworks to explode behind my closed eyes.

Startled once again into the present, I find myself rubbing the shiny patent leather of a collar, wondering what it might feel like against my throat and if you'd like it. I wonder what effect it might have, if any, on my cocksucking abilities. Selecting a thin, plain, black and red model, I pay for it and leave the store smiling.

THIS JUST IN

Heidi Champa

I couldn't believe I was finally walking into the newsroom for the first time. You had never wanted me to see where you work. You said it was too serious a place to goof around in. I hadn't argued with you, at least not too much. I was content to watch you on television, your image coming through my screen every night. It made me inexplicably horny watching you do the news. Almost every night, without fail, I would lie in bed and pleasure myself while watching you do your job.

Watching you staring at me and countless others through the camera lens made my body melt. I had never told you. Seeing you do it in person might have pushed me straight over the edge. But I still wanted to see it for myself. Be in the place I had visited so many times in my head but had never really seen.

I had seen your office, the tiny square room where you wrote and spent most of your time, but I had never had the chance to go to the studio. That was what I really wanted to see. In my head, I could see you sitting at your news desk reading to the world, while I hid underneath. No one would have to know what I was doing there. Only you would know. Many times, alone at night, I had secretly imagined kneeling under that stately desk, your cock straining and hardening in my mouth. You were so good, so professional, you probably wouldn't even miss a beat. Sure, in my fantasies you fucked me on the desk and over the desk. But I always wanted to be under it.

You pushed the door open and my eyes adjusted to the darkness. I looked at you, standing sheepishly with your hands in your pockets. After you motioned me in, I walked toward the desk I longed to see. I felt my pulse go up and a little bit of sweat form on my back. Standing on the empty and dark soundstage made it all seem so much less real. It didn't look how I had expected it to. It wasn't glamorous or even very interesting. It was an industrial space with a pretty face on it. It looked more like a garage than a news studio. Even the floor needed repair. The set hid the wires and lights and piles of garbage that the audience is never supposed to see. Just like the suit you put on every night, the set was just a nice covering for the real room. In front of the curtain and the backdrop of the set was your desk. Instead of being a real metal and glass fancy desk like I had thought, it was more of a mock-up of what a desk should look like. Behind the facade were shelves lined with your things; papers and mess were everywhere. Just like at home. I smiled as I looked at it, thinking *if only the world could see you as I do.* I heard your footsteps getting closer to me.

"I told you. It's not at all what it seems." You were standing next to the desk, leaning gently against its brittle frame. The few lights that were on barely showed me your face. You had your suit on for the broadcast but still had to go to makeup. It would be time for me to go soon. I sat down in the fake leather chair behind the desk. Looking out into the dark of the studio in front of me, I tried to imagine what it must feel like to command the room the way you do.

Just the sound of your voice, the vision of you on the screen was so reassuring to so many. You always tried to downplay the idea when I told you how much people liked you. Your modesty wouldn't let you believe it. But I heard it all the time from people who knew I was with you. The camera you look into sat in front of the desk, a big blank screen underneath ready to be filled with your words.

"Had enough yet? I have to get ready soon." I turned and looked at you. You were standing behind the chair with your arms folded. I realized that you would never get it. Never truly get how much you mattered. It made my heart swell just looking at you. My body flushed hot watching your uncomfortable eyes dart around the dark studio. You were impatient for me to go, but I couldn't have left if I wanted to. At least not yet.

"Sit down."

"Why?"

"Just humor me, okay?" I got up and you pulled out the chair and sat down. Instinctively sliding up to the desk, you straightened your jacket and your tie. I could almost see you doing that very thing while the whirl of activity moved around you in the studio. People calling out how much time was left before broadcast, how the lights looked, how the script sounded. All that, while you sat there and fixed your tie. Your calm came straight through the television and shot right into my pussy. And now, when I was standing in front of you in the dark, the effect was multiplied by a thousand. You noticed me staring, licking my lips, and you gave me a strange look.

"Why are you looking at me like that?"

"Like what?"

"Like you're ready to devour me." I didn't say anything, I

just took a few steps closer to you. You leaned back in your chair, regarding me with a puzzled look.

"I do want to devour you."

"Yeah, right. Okay. Listen, I have to go, so you'll have to leave."

You moved to stand up, but I pushed you back into your chair. You looked up at me with a face I had never seen before. "Stop fooling around. I have to get to makeup." I sank to my knees in front of your chair. I smiled at you, but you were still looking at me with aggravation. "Get up. I have to go."

I shook my head no. "There is one thing I want to do before I go." I reached up and took the paper script out of your pocket and set it on the desk in front of you. After smoothing out the papers that contained your rough drafts, I moved my hands to your zipper. You tried to stop me, stammering about work and begging me to be serious. But I didn't stop. Once my hand made its way into your boxers, your protests stopped.

"I want you to read. Read the news."

"What? Are you crazy? What is going on with you?"

"Just do it. Trust me." With a final smile, I turned your chair so you were facing the dark studio and the dormant camera. I slipped under the desk in front of you, and reached back into your pants. You hesitated, just sitting there. "Read, please." My fingers freed your cock from your boxers, and I heard your breath coming quick and erratic above me. You cleared your throat just as I stuck out my tongue to touch you. I heard your voice fill the empty space. I didn't care what you were talking about, I just wanted to hear your voice. I knew I could never have the real fantasy, that this was the closest I would ever get. You were hard, in spite of your clear discomfort. Even in an empty room, I could tell you were afraid of being caught. After all, this was your job. As the head of your cock eased back in my throat, the news of the day filled my ears. Your voice wobbled a bit, trying to adjust to the reality of me sucking you off at your desk. My hands ran up your thighs, pushing you deeper into my throat with each word that came out of your mouth.

"God, you're killing me." That wasn't on the page, but I was still happy to hear it.

Your voice was so warm. My fingers wrapped around the base of your cock, holding you deep in my throat for as long as I could. I ran my tongue up the shaft, and I heard you lose it for just a moment. The words had clearly been superseded by the feeling of my tongue sweeping up the ridge just below the head of your cock. But you kept on reading as I moved my tongue slowly up to suck the tip. God, I loved your cock so much. I had lost count of how many times I had sucked you off before. But nothing had felt as hot as this. I moved one hand from your leg and reached up under my skirt to find my panties nearly soaked through. Pushing them aside, I let two fingers slide slowly inside my pussy. I felt you looking down at me, heard you stop reading for just a few seconds. Without missing a beat, I looked up at you. Reluctantly letting your cock escape for a moment, I urged you on.

"Keep reading." You complied. Going back to your cock, I sucked the tip gently at first, then after a few swirls of the tongue, I took it all in my mouth again. I felt one of your hands drop to my head, guiding more than pushing me down. Despite my best efforts, you kept reading. I heard pages falling to the floor next to me, landing next to my knees. My fingers moved faster inside my pussy, as your cock moved faster in and out of my mouth. Both of your hands were on my head, urging me. Your voice was frantic, like nothing I had ever heard before. The words were tumbling out of your mouth faster and faster, but I didn't care. I just wanted to hear your voice. I felt my thighs start to tremble and I decided to slow things down just a little. I needed more, and I wanted you to have more before you came. I wanted you thinking about this as you were reading the news that night. Hell, I wanted you thinking about it every night.

I moved my hands back up to your thighs, running them over the Italian wool of your pants. Your fingers were twined in my hair as the last few pages of the news hit the floor with the others. You were harder than I had felt you in months. I wanted you deeper in my throat, and I never wanted to get up from under that desk. I wanted to be under there every night with you. "I can't take much more of this." That was all I needed to hear. My fingers dropped back to my pussy, and I felt your leg tremble under me as you pushed and pulled your cock in and out of my mouth. I wasn't in control anymore. You had gone back to running the show. Your show. I could feel you swelling, like you always did right before you came, but you didn't speed up like you usually did. Your pace was slow, each thrust deliberate and forceful. I felt the tip of your cock hit the back of my throat each time, shooting another electric shock straight to my pussy. I rubbed my clit with my thumb and felt everything start to unravel. My orgasm shouted through me but got trapped in my throat. I had to be content to moan around your cock, my fierce desire to yell turned into a few muffled hums. Your voice, on the other hand, was as powerful as ever. You cried out into the empty room, one last word from your beautiful lips. Aftershocks made you tremble as I felt you release your hands from my hair, and I felt your composure return.

Calm finally came back to the room, and I looked up at you. Your face was a picture of a million different emotions. You pushed back in your chair, and I retrieved your papers before I stood up. By the time I was done, you were buttoned up and looked every inch the professional newsman again. But I knew the truth. I kissed you, the shock still evident under your unflappable demeanor. "I should go, you have work to do." I walked out the door you had let me in and left you standing there.

That night, I knew, I wouldn't need to fantasize.

BLESSED BENEDICTION

Radclyffe

Every morning I get down on my knees and thank the powers that be that my girlfriend likes to get down on hers. She doesn't just like it, she loves it. She loves to give head. She doesn't care who knows it, either. This I know because I've heard her announce it more than once in the middle of a party when girls always seem to end up talking about sex.

"Danny has a gorgeous cock. I luvvvv to suck her off," my girl Shelby purrs.

She doesn't let on that she notices the raised eyebrows, some in question and others in disdain. She just lifts her chin and thrusts out her great tits and dares anyone to challenge her. No one ever does, so I wasn't expecting it when I walked up while she was making her usual pronouncement to three or four femmes at a late-night bash, and one of them, a haughty redhead, looked down her nose at Shelby and scoffed, "Oh, yeah. That I'd like to see."

Damn if one or two others didn't murmur in agreement.

"Hi, baby," I whispered, sliding up next to Shelby and nuzzling her ear. As I wrapped my arm around her waist, I nudged the stiff cock in my pants against her thigh. "Having a good time?"

She turned into me and looped her arms around my neck, rubbing against me the way she does when she wants to be sure she has my attention, while she pushed her tongue halfway down my throat. Being a few inches shorter, her soft belly molded to the ridge in the front of my jeans and when she rocked back and forth, she more than got my attention. She got my undying devotion and anything else she wanted.

"Unh," I muttered just to be sure she knew.

When she got done kissing me, she leaned back, her arms now draped loosely around my waist and her hips still slow-pumping between my legs and said, "These girls are in need of a demonstration. Do you mind?"

They say when your dick gets hard your brain gets soft, but a hard-on sure as hell doesn't make me stupid. I cupped her tight little ass in both hands and rubbed my rod up and down in the sweet divide between her thighs. "Whatever you say, baby."

Her eyes got all soft and liquid the way they do when she's getting turned on, and I knew my dick was doing its job, bumping her clit and making her wet. She curled her calf around the back of my thigh and ground into me until my legs started to shake. She could get me to the edge faster than a New York minute.

One of her girlfriends hooted and another one called challengingly, "So Shel, you gonna blow that cock, or fuck it?"

Shelby took a shuddering breath and pushed me backward until the backs of my knees hit a chair and I flopped down. My dick stood up like a rocket between my legs and screaming hot blood beat a crazy tattoo beneath it.

"Why don't you gather round and see for yourselves,"

Shelby said, talking to the femmes but watching me as she knelt between my thighs.

Oh, yeah, blessed, blessed be.

Now, the reason my girl is such a great cocksucker is that she understands that a blow job is as much about the show as it is about her hot, wet mouth sliding up and down my cock until I come in her mouth. She doesn't go down on me like it's a chore, or penance, or a favor. She turns giving head into a work of art. Every move is designed to let me know she gets off on my cock, and that teasing my rod makes her cream.

"You want me to suck you, baby?" Shelby murmured, scraping her nails down my fly. The vibration hit me where I live and my hips twitched.

"Yeah," I croaked. Fuck, just thinking about what she was gonna do to me twisted my insides into a knot. "Take it out."

She smiled and jerked me a little, the tip of her tongue gliding slowly between her lips. "Sure?"

"Come on, babe. Suck my cock." I sounded pathetic now, but I didn't care. A hard-on leaves no room for pride.

She laughed and the show began.

I love to watch her take my cock out. She never hurries; in fact, sometimes she works me around inside my pants for so long, by the time she gets me in her hand I'm ready to blow like a first-timer the minute she tongues me. She popped the button on my jeans and pulled my T-shirt out. With her eyes still on mine, she rubbed my belly and kissed my cock through my jeans. I gripped the arms of the chair and lifted my hips, pushing my cock against her face. One of her girlfriends leaned against the side of the chair and draped her arm over the back, her fingertips grazing my neck. Her breast just skimmed my shoulder. Another one in a skirt so short I could see a pale pink scrap of silk covering her pussy crowded up on the opposite side. The bitchy redhead leaned down from behind Shelby and skimmed Shelby's long blonde hair back from her face so everyone could see as Shelby mouthed my cock. The faded denim over the head of my dick was soaked from her sucking on it.

"Are you getting nice and hard for me?" Shelby asked, running her fingers up and down the bulge in my jeans.

I humped her hand, jacking myself up good. "Locked and loaded."

She gave my cock a swat and warned, "Don't even think about shooting until I tell you you can."

I just nodded dumbly as she tugged down my fly. My white briefs, stretched taut over my straining cock, heaved out through the gap.

"Ooo," one of Shelby's girlfriends said breathily. "I'd like to see you deep-throat that monster, honey."

"Just watch," Shelby replied and slid her dainty fist inside my jockeys.

"Uh," I grunted, my vision going double as she wrapped her fingers around me and gave me a couple of quick pumps just to be sure I was ready for her.

Then she twisted her wrist left, then right, and pulled my cock out into the air. A good three inches stuck out past her fist, which she kept wrapped around the base. With her eyes locked on mine, she kissed the tip and swirled her tongue around the head.

"The thing about boys," Shelby said to her friends, pausing every now and then to lick the underside of my cock, "is that all they think about is shooting that load." She slid her fist up my wet cock until only the head was visible. "A really good blow job takes time, so don't let them rush you."

She made a circle of her ruby red lips and sucked the fat, shiny tip into her mouth. At the same time, she skimmed her fist down my rod. Pressure surged between my legs and I mumbled something stupid like, *Oh, yeah, suck my dick*, like she wasn't already doing it. She hummed a happy sound and slid another inch or two in her mouth and my legs started a little dance. Up. Down. Up. Down.

"Fuck," I muttered, because I was about to embarrass myself in front of all these girls.

"Now," Shelby said, letting my cock pop out of her mouth, "if you jack their cock and suck at the same time, they'll last about thirty seconds." While she talked, she kissed and licked the head of my dick and jiggled the shaft back and forth over the spot where she knew I was stiff and pulsing. "That's fine if you're doing them while they're driving or you wake up with their hard-on in your face and you haven't even had coffee yet. Then a fast jerk and blow works great, doesn't it, baby?"

Just watching her tongue flick at the head of my dick was making my belly tingle and I was close to letting loose even if she wasn't jacking me off. "I want to come in your mouth."

Shelby laughed and looked up at her girlfriends. "See? One-track mind."

"Suck her cock," the redhead ordered, her voice all tight like something hurt her.

"Yeah, make her pop," the one in the short skirt standing next to me muttered, and I caught a glimpse of a wet spot in the middle of her pale pink panties.

"Be good, baby," Shelby murmured, and then she really got down to business.

Inch by inch, she sucked my cock into her mouth until her lips met the circle of her thumb and index finger around the base of my shaft. Then she slowly slid all the way back to the crown, following her mouth with her hand. When she got to the end, she circled her tongue around the head and toyed with the tip before sliding her lips and hand back down again. My cock was slick from the wetness of her mouth, making it easier for her to jerk me off.

"You like that, babe?" I whispered, clasping the back of her head with my hand. I knew better than to force her down on it, but I liked to feel her moving up and down on me. She rolled her eyes up to mine, her mouth full of my cock, and I read her answer in her glassy unfocused gaze. Knowing she got off sucking me off is what really did it for me. "You like my big cock down your throat?"

She pulled off long enough to mumble, "I love your cock," and then she slurped me down again.

Watching her lids get heavy and her cheeks flutter as she sucked and licked and worked me in her fist stoked the fire between my legs. I felt that coiled-spring-about-to-snap tension deep down inside and I couldn't help it, I had to fuck her mouth.

"You're gonna make me come," I gasped, my stomach tight as a board. "Suck it, baby, suck it. Suck it."

She picked up her pace, her hand and mouth a blur on my cock, the sound of her wet tongue lapping at me like thunder in my ears. She knew just how to grind my cock over the hard center of my need, and I grabbed her head in both hands, getting ready to shoot.

One of her girlfriends reached down and rubbed my belly. "Oh, damn, girl, she's about to unload right down your throat."

Shelby whimpered, her mouth too full for anything else, and my cock and my clit exploded. I yelled and my hips jumped, and Shelby pulled back just enough so I didn't choke her. She didn't let up on me though, sucking and stroking until I collapsed in the chair, my arms and legs limp and useless.

She sat back on her heels and licked her lips, still slow-stroking my cock. She gazed up at her girlfriends, who all looked flushed and hot. "The best thing about sucking her off," Shelby said sweetly, "is that now she's not in so much of a hurry." She stood, hiked up her skirt and twitched her panties aside, and straddled my hips. Her eyes shuttered closed for a second as she took me deep, then she shuddered and sighed. "So she can fuck me just as long as I need her to."

And me? Hell, after a blow job like that, she can have anything she wants. Hallelujah.

HOW I LEARNED TO GIVE GOOD HEAD

Amanda Earl

Yes, I met him online, and to be honest I wasn't all that attracted to him, but it was almost New Year's Eve and I didn't have any plans. The snow was already falling hard here in Ottawa. My downtown bachelorette apartment was closing in on me. It was my first holiday season alone. In my new life as a single woman, I set out to be bold and sexually adventurous. I packed my sheer black stockings, a red lace garter, a matching push-up bra, some condoms, a small bottle of travel lube, and not much else. I took the bus to Montreal, where he met me at the station.

His name was Stephen. He was short by my standards, maybe five-six. His eyes were hazel. I like tall men, long hair, and any eye color but hazel. Still, he'd charmed me into taking a two-hour trip on a bleak wintry afternoon in order to meet him, a man I didn't know. That meant he had some talent. I was curious enough to discover what it was.

Was there chemistry between us? Not really. He made me pay

for the cab by convincing me he would pay for dinner that night. I had just forked over fifty dollars on a round-trip bus ticket, so I was already a tad cynical. But I paid.

His apartment was early twenty-first-century barren with almost no furnishings to speak of. There were no bookshelves and no books. I'm immediately suspicious of people who don't own books. How do they spend their time? How do they escape from the drudgery of reality?

In his living room, we sat on the couch for a few minutes and kissed. It was okay. I was still somewhat immersed in the idea of my adventurous sexy self, so I took my role seriously and used my best kissing techniques, tongue over lips, gentle feathery kisses, bottom lip suck, et cetera.

One of the things that had bonded us online was that he loved to receive oral sex and I loved to give it, so it wasn't long before he had his pants off and I was on the floor at his crotch, licking and sucking.

"Not bad," he said, "but I can teach you a few things that men will thank me for later."

I love arrogance in a man. I suppose I should have felt insulted, but I've always loved to learn. Let me tell you that no man so far had complained about my oral abilities. I let them all go as deep as they wanted down my throat and licked them for a good long time. After a while my jaw got tired or we simply became interested in other things; sometimes they came down my throat, but that didn't happen too often. Perhaps I did have something to learn, after all.

I looked up at Stephen and nodded. He placed my right hand around his shaft. His prick wasn't particularly large or thick, which was fine. It was your standard six incher with a graceful dusky purple head.

"The important thing is to use your hands," he said. "Then

get the big fellow nice and wet with your tongue and mouth. That's right, take it in your mouth," he urged.

I slipped his penis between my lips and started to deep-throat it.

"No, just the head, hon."

I backed off and wet his cockhead with my tongue.

"Now move your hand up and down the pole and let the wetness run down over the whole thing, baby."

I followed his commands, getting turned on by being ordered and at the same time wondering if he still remembered my name. He cupped my head with his hand and guided me in rhythm to his strokes as his cock moved in and out of my mouth.

"Make your lips nice and slack. Move your hand in time to the strokes, honey."

He was sounding more and more urgent. Still my rhythm was staccato. I looked up into his eyes again, worried that I wasn't making the grade. He put his hands around my hand and stroked, getting me to follow his rhythm.

"Now lick the rim," he whispered, and I did, letting my tongue follow round and round the head, round and round, round and round, as we pistoned his cock in and out of my mouth, the saliva and precome running down onto my face and chest.

He backed off and I felt disappointed.

"You haven't earned the right to swallow my come, sweetheart."

He stood up and jerked off while he looked down upon me and soon the come shot out and all over my face. I was exceptionally turned on; my cunt was soaked. I wanted more, but I wasn't getting it.

He went to the bathroom to clean up and then let me go in there too, but only after he was done. I didn't have long before he shouted out to me that we were going out to dinner. My legs were still shaky, but I was hungry and looking forward to what I imagined would be a sumptuous dinner in Montreal. I didn't have time to don my sexy undergarments for the adventure.

We walked a few blocks to a Chinese restaurant that was, like his apartment, quite bare. I swear that nothing on the menu was over ten dollars. He ordered us a big bowl of soup, very thin on the meat, with a few slices of green onion on top for decoration. I tried not to calculate that this meal would cost him about half the amount I'd paid for the cab. My mouth was still tired from the sucking anyway.

After dinner we walked to a nearby video store where he picked out two videos, not asking me what I'd like. One was some Disney film, which struck me as odd, and the other some Cheech and Chong–like, buddies-on-the-road movie that sounded dull.

We went a bit farther, walking in the deep snow of Montreal streets. I was surprised to see a woman feeding pigeons in the snow. She'd dug a bit of an indentation and placed seed on top. Stephen, for some reason, decided to stop and help her pour the feed from a big bag of seed. We watched while the pigeons swooped down through the snow, cooing and jockeying for position as they pecked up the seed. I felt happy to witness Stephen's unexpected generosity and hopeful for the evening to come.

We walked on farther at a rapid pace. My legs were really sore from the heavy snow and the pace and the fact that I'd spent the better part of an hour on my knees shortly before our excursion. We stopped at a grocery store where Stephen bought a big sack of oranges. Then we went back to his place.

He gently placed everything on a chair by the door, including his clothes. I stripped and left my clothes on the floor, which he took no notice of. Then he kissed me, and led me into his dark bedroom. He didn't turn on the lights, just sat on the edge of the bed. I took my position once more on the floor at his feet and watched as he touched himself. While he stroked he continued the lesson:

"I want to feel every movement of your mouth on my cock, each loosening and tightening of your lips. Make my cock wet. Use your tongue in the slit, lick around the rim, up and down the shaft...warm and wet. Change your rhythm, fast and slow."

He slid his swollen cock into my mouth. I squeezed his shaft and my tongue traced the slit.

"Turn that mouth into a cunt. I want to feel like my dick is being fucked by the tightest, most responsive cunt ever known."

I let my fingers play along the sac as it grew tighter. My lips tightened around the cockhead, wetting it, while my hands encircled the rod and moved in rhythm to the way he'd been stroking himself, a kind of quick four-four-time step with penis and hand and mouth acting as the orchestra.

"Give me a little teeth now, hon."

I took more of him into my mouth until his cock caught on one of my back molars. He took a ragged breath and kept pumping.

"Swallow it. Clutch those hot lips around my shaft and tease up and down. Go faster now, faster, honey. "

I sucked more into my mouth, gently tugging on it. He moaned as I sucked and licked and fondled.

"That's it, baby, so warm, so wet, so tight. Don't stop."

He touched my head and pushed me in closer. I nuzzled the hair above his cock, licked just below his stomach, leaned in close to inhale the musky scent of him and then sucked the head into my mouth again, warming him with my hot breath.

"That feels so fucking good."

He looked down at me and into my eyes. I felt his hardness

throbbing in my mouth. I knew he was going to come soon. I opened my mouth wider and pressed my breasts against the tops of his thighs. Then I moved back and he pushed me away and once again came on my chest and face. My legs were weak and shaky. After he was done, I rose.

"Maybe next time, I'll come down your throat, babe. Clean up and we'll watch some videos."

Part of me was wondering why in heck I'd made the trip to Montreal to meet him. Still though, I knew my technique was improving. When I came out of the bathroom, he took his turn. I dressed and headed back into the living room, looking out at the snow still falling.

The Disney movie turned out to be this hockey movie that he had a part in as an extra. It was shot out West, somewhere in Saskatchewan. The film was dull, and I found myself dozing in the chair as I watched Stephen peel and eat orange after orange. He did offer me one, which I ate, worrying a bit that perhaps Stephen was a crazy man.

After the next film, he suggested we go to bed and off we went. He turned on the light. The curtains were white and sheer, the bedspread was a white duvet cover, and everything in the room was white. He told me not to get the cover dirty, turned out the light, and promptly fell asleep, his body curled away from mine. I watched the snow fall in the glare of the streetlight. I was completely surrounded by white, a pristine new white. This was the way I would end the old year, a year that had begun with the end of my marriage and was ending in bed beside this stranger, this strange man.

The next morning he invited me to watch as he took a bath. We went into the bathroom, I sat on the toilet, and he bathed. There were all kinds of products on a shelf in the corner of the stall. He even had a bottle of bleach. I watched while he carefully scrubbed himself down and used various products on his body. After he was done, he suggested I bathe also, but he didn't stay to watch.

I didn't linger in the tub too long, and came out wrapped in one of his sterilized towels. I found him sitting on the bed and I knew what he expected. I took my place on the floor and licked him once more. This time I didn't take him into my mouth right away. I licked and stroked, I encircled his shaft and placed it against my breasts. I tantalized him with every movement. The sun lit the whiteness of the room so that it was a brilliant, blinding white. When I took his cock into my mouth, I looked up at him and into his eyes and smiled. I knew I was going to make this man come. And I knew it didn't have to do so much with his lessons as it did with my own realization that I could do anything I wanted to do. I'd made a decision to ring in the New Year with this stranger. I was free. And I'd learned something in the bargain. Something I would show a more deserving man in the new year.

"Happy New Year," I said to myself, as his come shot down my throat.

WITHOUT EYES

Terri Pray

Susan paced across the bedroom, her heart racing. He was late. He was never late, so what was going on? He always called if something went wrong and he'd been delayed, so where was he? She glanced at the clock for the tenth time in the past twenty minutes. This just wasn't like him. Had he been in an accident?

The sound of the car pulling into the driveway silenced her fears, for now at least, and turned them into something else. Anger. If he was all right, why hadn't he called to let her know he'd be late?

"Susan?" he called out, the door slamming shut behind him. "Where are you?"

"Up here." *Up here steaming and about ready to explode!* No, she couldn't tell him that. Keep calm, keep focused, and don't let him see just how angry she was. There'd be a perfectly good explanation as to why he was late. She had to believe that.

Tom smiled as he walked into the bedroom, holding a black

and green plastic bag. "I brought something home for us."

Shopping? He'd been shopping? "Where the hell have you been, I've been worried sick!"

He blinked and took a step back. "Where did that come from?"

"You're late. You always call if you're going to be late. In five years you've never missed calling me. I've been worried out of my mind."

He flushed, then paled, looking away, the bag shifting from one hand to the other. "I'm sorry, I just got distracted. I had this idea and well…"

"You didn't think!" Her hands itched. She'd never felt more tempted to smack him in her entire life. "You were thoughtless and didn't stop to think how I'd feel!"

"Hey, I said I was sorry."

"Do you think that makes me feel any better?"

His gaze narrowed as he tossed the bag onto the bed. "I had something planned for us both, but right now it looks like you need a lesson in respect. Or have you forgotten just who is in charge of this household?"

Her heart skipped a beat and she lowered her hands to her sides. "I'm sorry, I wasn't thinking straight, sir."

"I should put you over my knee, but I have a better idea. One that will remind you of your place, my girl." He tapped one hand against his thigh. "Go and shower, settle your mind, and return to me."

Susan let out a long, slow breath. She'd gotten off lightly and she knew it, but still, she'd had a reason to be angry with him and maybe he'd taken that into account. "Yes, sir, and I'm sorry. I was just worried and then angry. I'll try to do better."

"Yes, you will." The warning was all too clear in his voice.

She cursed herself as she turned and walked out of the

bedroom into the bathroom, turning the shower on and closing the door. This was one of the few places where she was permitted a little privacy. Now she wasn't sure if she'd be allowed to keep the door closed after the way she'd spoken to him.

A long shower. Maybe that would help? It couldn't hurt. At least this way she could relax and forget her tension.

Steam curled upward, seeping over the top of the shower curtain, and she dropped her clothing into the basket before stepping into the warm water. She closed her eyes before turning her head into the water, enjoying the heated massage of wet fingers that played across her face.

Less than five minutes later she stepped out of the shower and wrapped a thick, warm towel about her body. It had helped. The hot water had washed away some of her tension, and she now felt ready to face him. She only hoped he wasn't still angry with her—not that she wouldn't have deserved it if he was.

With the towel dropped into the laundry hamper she walked out of the bathroom and into the bedroom and knelt at the foot of the bed, her thighs spread, hands lightly placed on her still damp legs, her gaze lowered. A soft tremble washed through her body, her nerves threatening to get the better of her. She'd lost her temper, something she'd struggled with for years. Even though she'd had good reason, she knew better. She knew how to handle it. Ask instead of demand. Ranting and raving only meant she'd failed.

"I was angry with you, when you snapped at me, but I know that it was partially my fault. I do normally call and you were worried because I don't, normally, change my habits. However, the fact that you snapped does show that you need a reminder of just who is in charge in this house." His voice was calm as he spoke, standing naked in their room. The play box stood open at the side of the bed.

"Yes, sir. I'm sorry, I should have found a way to control my temper."

"Stand."

Susan moved to her feet quickly.

"Hands behind your back."

She swallowed hard and crossed her wrists in the small of her back.

"Don't move until I tell you otherwise." He bent over, picking up two items from the play box before he walked behind her. Soft cuffs were locked on her wrists, holding them in place. She trembled even as he checked the cuffs, knowing that she would be forbidden the use of her hands for whatever he had in mind.

Then he bound the blindfold about her eyes, stealing her sight.

"You will serve me, like this, and perhaps remember some of our early days together when you strove to find a way to please me. You've forgotten how it felt then, how you needed to do your best—this will remind you." He pulled her back a step from the bed and moved in front of her, sitting down on the edge of the bed. "Your mouth, lips, tongue, cheeks; all of these you will use to please me. Is that understood?"

"Yes, sir." Her stomach knotted.

"Then do it."

Susan lowered slowly to her knees, edging closer to him as she felt him part his thighs so she could ease between them. Her breasts brushed against his inner thighs as she settled herself into position. Her nipples crinkled into hardened points, her breath catching in the back of her throat. His presence filled her senses, his aroma tempting her closer. Without her sight, everything else became sharper.

"That's it, find your way. You know how to please me. Use that knowledge now."

Normally she used her hands. This time she couldn't; she couldn't stroke his inner thighs like she was used to.

But she could kiss them.

She twisted, lowering her head a little more, suddenly aware of how her hair brushed his thighs and the way he quivered at the touch. Susan pressed her lips against his inner thigh, kissing softly, feeling the play of muscles beneath his skin as she began to lick and nibble her way inward.

He groaned, the low sound urging her onward.

She took her time: Tasting him. Licking. Tracing the tip of her tongue over his skin in long, slow, swirls.

"Yes, that's it, my girl."

His. She'd been his for many years now and would always be his.

His cock thickened, brushing against her cheek as she worked her way slowly in. His erection throbbed, the scent of his arousal filled her nose, his heavy sac hung close, touching her chin as she turned her head to lick, softly, across the length of his cock. It took her a moment before she could find and capture the head of his cock in her lips, but she managed it, and groaned at the taste, his arousal coating the smooth skin, seeping into her mouth as she drew it in a little at a time, licking, suckling his cock.

"Yes." The word was little more than a hiss from the man she loved and had submitted to years ago.

A wicked smile claimed her lips. Slow. She'd take this slow. Tease him. Torment him. Show him everything she'd learned about him. Just because she was submissive didn't mean that, even now with her hands bound and her sight stolen, she didn't have the power. Especially now.

She flicked her tongue rapidly across the head of his cock, sucking hard until she felt a deep rocking work through his hips, then she pulled back, opening her mouth and letting his cock slide out between her lips, over her tongue.

"Hey—what are you up to?" His words were a groan, his cock pressing against her cheek as she turned her head to seek out his other thigh with her lips.

Susan didn't speak; instead she scraped her teeth carefully over the tender skin of his inner thigh. His thigh shook, his breath catching, his body tense as she nipped and licked her way back to his knee, moving away from his cock and the center of his desire.

"Wicked wench."

Yes, I am.

"You know what I want."

Yes, I do.

"Teasing me. You'll pay for it, of course."

Counting on it. She licked around his knee and knelt up, arching her back. With her hands bound behind her back, she knew the position would lift her breasts up for him, displaying her body for his view. Not enough; she could do more, she knew that. Slowly, carefully, she lifted up from her heels, tipping her hips, swaying them softly from side to side, circling them deeply as she danced on her knees for him.

His thighs tightened on either side of her body. "Susan..."

"Don't you like what you see, sir?"

"Yes, but..."

"Then let me please you. It's what you told me to do."

He couldn't argue with that one and fell silent.

Slowly, she turned her body, never moving from her knees, stretching, arching, her hips dancing, never ceasing the sensual patterns. Her skin heated, her core rippling as she moved, knowing what her dance was doing to him. The sight of her nude, bound, and blindfolded form writhing for him, only for him, aroused him. She didn't need to see him to know that.

His breathing became ragged; his thighs tensed on either side of her body. Any moment now she expected him to reach for her and drag her down until her mouth was forced back onto his cock. But she was in control here. She would show him just how well his wife knew him.

Just when she thought she had pushed too far, she stopped and lowered down once more, edging back in, nuzzling her way to his groin. Her hair brushed over his cock and balls, teasing them; she blew against his balls, taking care not to catch the head of his cock, then tickled over his heavy sac with the tip of her tongue. He groaned above her, his hips rolling, hunger clear in his body.

Now.

Susan licked softly around his sac, feeling his balls tighten within the soft skin. Then she moved slowly upward, tracing the tip of her tongue over his sac until she found the base of his cock. It throbbed beneath her gentle touch. Heat coated her inner walls. She knew, by the time she had brought him to his release, she would be aching for his touch in return.

She had to focus on him, not on her own desires right now.

Her lips closed around the tip of his cock, his taste heady as she swept her tongue over the smooth surface, dipping into his slit, tasting him deeply. His thick cock throbbed in her mouth; his hips rolled, sliding farther into her mouth as she wrapped her tongue around his needful erection.

Susan purred into his cock, feeling the vibrations play from her mouth directly onto him; the reaction was instantaneous. Tom's fingers slid into her hair, fisting, holding her tight. His hips rolled, thrusting deep into her mouth, taking her, his balls slapping against her chin.

She relaxed, her throat welcoming his cock as he claimed her mouth. *Soon, so soon.* Only now did she realize the tables had turned. She was helpless. In his grasp. She couldn't stop him: Bound. Blindfolded. Gagged with his cock, but she welcomed this, knowing she'd driven him to this point. Her touches, her knowledge, had forced him to the brink of self-control.

"God!" he cried out above her, his thrusts harder than before, his grip in her hair almost painful, but she didn't care. "Going to…"

His taste, then—thick, hot, ropey threads of his salty orgasm flooded her mouth, forcing her to swallow. Only when he shuddered and finally eased back from her lips could she take a clear breath. Silent, trembling, she knelt at the foot of the bed, his grip no longer in her hair. Her body was coated in small beads of sweat; her inner walls rippling, coated with her own need, but she knew if that was to be sated, it would be at his desire, his whim, not hers.

This was the life she had chosen. The life she had welcomed.

He brushed the back of his fingers over her cheek, his voice husky. "Well done, mine."

Susan leaned into his touch, his words wrapping around her heart in a loving cocoon. This was the life she still desired with him.

TONY TEMPO

Tsaurah Litzky

I never thought I'd end up like this, spending my final years in the Crescendo Home for Aged and Indigent Musicians. Yet here I am—Tony Tempo, once know as the trumpet king of swing. I'm heading toward that last command performance watching "Jeopardy!" with a bunch of wizened old music makers in the common room of a converted Victorian mansion in Baldwin, Long Island.

I thought I'd spend my old age with my darling Clara, my high school honey, my wife of forty-five years. I was sure she'd outlive me, me with my daily pack of Pall Malls and nightly half-bottle of Jack, but then she up and died. An embolism, the doctor called it, a bubble of blood popped, burst in her brain. He said it didn't hurt her, she just saw red and then she was gone forever.

I had hoped we'd head south when I retired, move to Florida. After she kicked the bucket, I didn't retire. I hung on, kept touring, playing my trumpet, but wherever I was, whatever song I was playing, she was always on my mind. A couple of years ago, I had this stroke. I lost all the feeling and movement in my right leg. Now I'm an old gimp on a walker. At least I can still play my trumpet; at least I still got my memories, my imagination.

I used to imagine Clara and me in Florida. We'd buy a nice condominium by the sea. In the afternoons, I'd play shuffleboard on the boardwalk while she sat on the balcony of our condo reading those romance novels she loved. We'd eat dinner in a fancy restaurant, then walk on the beach holding hands. After that, we'd go home and make love. Clara was always so hot for me; we partied every night until the day she died.

I'd lie in bed on top of the covers stripped to my birthday suit while Clara was taking her shower. She'd come out of the bath-room naked as Venus rising from the sea. She was voluptuous, a va-va-voom girl, with boobs big and round as bowling balls. Her hips were wide and welcoming. From across the room, I could smell the sweet honey in her snatch. Just the sight of her made my horn stand up high as one of those rockets at Cape Canaveral. She would wiggle slowly toward me, doing a dance older than time.

She'd lick her lips, moistening them, and then bend over my bare belly and take me in her mouth of a thousand delights. Her lips and tongue were always so wet that every time she went down on me I felt like I was floating in a lake of love. She'd cover my cock-a-doodle with kisses, caress it up and down with her flickering tongue.

Clara loved to smoke my pipe, as she called it. She had this trick, something she did with her head, twisting it round and round in a corkscrew motion when she had her tongue on me. It never failed to get me so worked up I was about to explode. She usually stopped before that could happen, to let me calm down.

She'd lick her way up through my coarse crotch hair, trace that tongue past my navel to my chest, find my nipple and nurse there until it hardened into a little diamond. All the while she would be holding me, her fingers curled around my equipment like a prayer. She always knew the exact right moment to lick her way back down south and suck me again.

How I miss her. There're no women here except the nurses, and they treat us like babies. For example, Miss Pouty, when she knocks on my door every day at three p.m., says the same thing. Her voice is loud and syrupy, oozing with heartburn: "Would Tony like a little snacky-poo?" What I'd really like is a snacky-poo on some poontang, but I don't tell her that as I silently open the door and accept the milk and cookies she offers. She is maybe five feet tall and five feet around, with a slight mustache. It's painful to imagine her in a flimsy see-through negligee, but I know she is a woman, a human being, and must have desires like everyone else. One day I decide to have a little fun, kid around with her, maybe lighten things up.

When she knocks on my door, I hobble over and open it. I make as much of a gallant bow as I can manage.

"Good afternoon, Miss Pouty," I say.

She draws back, surprised, and she doesn't seem pleased. I've upset our usual routine. "Would Mr. Tony like a little snacky-poo?' she asks, but now her saccharine voice has a sharp edge. I give her what I hope is a winning smile; too bad I don't have my dentures in.

"I'd rather snack on your luscious lips," I answer. She steps back, nearly drops the tray. Her complexion turns from pale gray to angry orange. "What's the matter with you?" she sputters. "You're too old to even think about such things. You're obviously showing symptoms of dementia. Try any funny stuff, buster, and I'll fix you so you won't even be able to change your own diapers." She slams the door and I hear her clomping away down the hall. I don't even wear diapers and she has hurt my feelings. So much for a little innocent flirtation.

I feel shaky, so I totter back across the room and sink down on my bed. She may think that all I have left between my legs is a skinny straw to piss through. Little does she know my sleep is filled with dreams of Clara. Every morning I wake up with my hand holding a hard-on the size of a beer can, or a poor boy. The wall above my headboard is covered with pictures and mementos from my career, but the other wall, along the side of my bed, is covered with photos of Clara. When I open my eyes, I have forty Claras to look at. My favorite picture is of her wearing the red two-piece bathing suit with ruffles I brought her in 1980 when we were vacationing on the French Riviera. She was no longer young but she still looked like a rose. Every morning, I imagine Clara kneeling between my legs in that bathing suit. She has me deep in her throat, her hands cupping my nuts, her head bobbing up and down. Sometimes I come two times in a row.

A couple of nights after the Miss Pouty incident, I'm feeling low. My gut is all churned up; maybe I ate too much of that chili lasagna at dinner. I don't leaf through my old sheet music or practice the scales on my trumpet like I often do in the evenings. Instead, I shut off the lights, climb into bed, and pull the covers over my head.

I imagine Clara lying beside me without a stitch on. All she's wearing is the black leather mask she puts on when she wants me to take her in the ass. There is a loud knock. It must be ten o'clock, time for my nighttime meds. I hope it isn't grouchy Miss Pouty.

"Come in," I call.

"May I switch on the light?" a sweet voice, certainly not Miss Pouty's, asks hesitantly. "Sure," I say. The lights go on, and standing in my doorway is a little woman with a nice face. She cuts a trim figure in her nurse's uniform, first nurse I've seen around here who has a waist. "I'm your new night nurse, Mary," she says. "May I come in?"

"Yes, ma'am," I answer and I sit straight up in bed. She smiles at me as she steps into the room. She has a grin that would melt a snowman's heart.

"According to my chart, you're Tempo, Tony Tempo." Her big eyes take in the pictures, the framed album covers on the wall.

Those big eyes grow even wider. "You're *the* Tony Tempo," she says, her voice rising, "who played with the Harvest Moon Orchestra and with Bucky Bernstein's Big Band! You made the record *Trumpet Solos for Love*. My father had all your records but he loved that one best. When I was real little, he liked to put it on the record player. He'd wrap one arm around my mama's waist, gather me up in his other arm, and we'd all waltz around together. Oh, Mr. Tempo, I can't believe I'm actually meeting you."

"Call me Tony," I say. Her glance falls on my walker.

"Mr. T—I mean, Tony, I see from your chart that you had a stroke. Do you still play the trumpet?"

"I do," I tell her. "Maybe I'll play a tune for you."

"Could you play 'Begin the Beguine'? That's my favorite." That was Clara's favorite too.

"No problem, I'd be delighted," I say.

"Right now?" she asks hopefully. Then she looks at her watch and frowns. Her lips are so shiny and red and she isn't even wearing any lipstick.

"I forgot," she says. "Head nurse told me you're not supposed to play music after ten o'clock. Some of the other residents are sleeping by then."

The stiffy between my legs is perking up. I puddle the blanket over my legs so she won't see. "Don't worry," I tell her. "I hope to perform for you soon."

"I look forward to that," she says as she hands me my pills.

"When are you coming back?" I ask her before she leaves.

"Tomorrow night," she answers, then clicks off the light and goes out the door.

By eight o'clock the next night, I'm freshly shaved. What is left of my hair is parted on one side and neatly combed. I usually spend the day in a sweatshirt and sweatpants but I have changed into the clean white shirt and clean chinos that were hanging in my closet. My trumpet is in its usual place, resting in the case on top of the dresser.

At eight-thirty by the clock, there's a knock on the door. "Come in," I say.

"Good evening, Tony," she greets me. "I came to you first. It's still early enough for you to play me a song." She looks like a sunny day. I know I'm being an idiot. Why should a pretty woman like her be interested in an old fart like me? Is she just trying to be nice or is she genuinely interested in the music? It doesn't matter, I'm just happy to see her.

"I was hoping you might show up early, because I had the same idea. Sit down, make yourself comfortable," I tell her as I shuffle over to get the trumpet.

She sits down on the bed and puts the tray of pills beside her. I notice she isn't wearing a wedding ring. "Tell me, Mary," I ask as I unlatch the case. "How come you're working nights? Don't you have a family?" She looks down at her hands, which are twisting in her lap.

"My husband and I split up years ago," she says. "My son is still in school and busy with his friends. I like working nights. It keeps me from being lonely."

"It's hard to be alone," I agree. "My wife's been gone ten

years. I miss her all the time. There's pictures of her on the wall behind you."

Mary turns her head and takes a look. "She's so pretty," she says.

"You're pretty, too," I respond. Did I imagine it or did her face get a tinge of pink?

She looks up at me expectantly. I pick up the trumpet, put in the mouthpiece, and start to blow. The notes come out perfect, golden. I can hear Ella singing those romantic words about palms swaying and rapture serene. I never played better. A woman can sure bring out the best music in a man. Playing for Mary, I almost feel like a kid again. Her mouth is half-open, her eyes half-shut. She seems enthralled. When I am done, she claps her hands.

"Oh, Tony, you sound even better than on the record," she says. "It's been so long since I've heard live music. Play another for me?"

"With great pleasure," I tell her. "I'll take requests from the audience."

"Hmm," she says. "Let me think." She leans back, crosses her legs. They are very shapely, even in their shiny white nurse's hose and clunky nurse's oxfords. "How about 'Lover Man'?" she asks, batting her thick, dark eyelashes.

I nearly drop my horn. Can she be flirting with me? I try to be cool, control the sudden shaking in my fingers. "This one is dedicated to Mary," I say as if we were in a big nightclub. Once again each note is perfect; the melody floats in the air like a kiss. This time Mary doesn't clap. She jumps up, put her arms around me, and gives me a big, soft smooch on the cheek. She smells of rubbing alcohol and Dentyne.

"Tony, when you play it makes me so happy," she whispers against my shoulder.

"It makes me feel like dancing."

"Dancing tomorrow night," I tell her.

"Okay," she says. "I'll try to come early again."

The next night, I am ready and waiting for her by 7:30. I even put on some Old Spice cologne from a bottle that must have been sitting in my bathroom cabinet for two years. When she finally knocks, my heartbeat races like a metronome. *Get a grip,* I tell myself, *or you'll welcome her with a heart attack.* I take a couple of deep breaths. "Come in," I call.

"Hi," Mary says, stepping into the room. "How are you tonight, Tony?"

I decide to go for broke. "Right as rain, now that you're here, Mary," I tell her.

She giggles. "You make me feel so special," she says.

"You are special," I answer. "Come sit down on the bed and we'll chat awhile."

She sits down on the bed and puts the medicine tray beside her like the last time. She is pale and has dark circles under her eyes. "You look a little beat. You working too hard?" I ask.

"No," she says, "it's kind of you to ask. It's my son; he's fallen in with a bad crowd. I don't know what to do."

"I hope you don't mind me giving you some advice?" I ask.

"Please," she tells me. "I'm ready to pull my hair out."

"You need to sit down with him and talk to him straight," I suggest. "Tell him he only lives once and if he starts to screw up, it's hard to get back on track. How old is he?"

"Twenty," she says. I'm surprised. I thought her kid would still be in grade school.

I make a joke. "When did you have him, when you were fifteen?" Her face perks up a little.

"I'm fifty now, Tony," she tells me. I had thought she was in her early forties.

"Well then," I say. "You're just the right age for me." She doesn't say yes, she doesn't say no. She suddenly leans over and kisses me right on the mouth, a lingering kiss full of promises. I kiss her back. I am glad I still remember how to do it. When her lips part, I slide my tongue in. The wood is growing up so high between my legs I'm afraid I'll poke her in her full bosom. Then she starts sucking on my tongue and I stop being frightened of anything.

"I'm feeling so much better," Mary says when we pull apart. The way I'm sitting makes my knee push against the walker standing next to the bed.

"I know I promised you dancing, Mary," I tell her, trying to keep any hint of bitterness out of my voice, "but even with this contraption, I don't know if I could manage a two-step."

"I don't care. I like to be with you. You're still an attractive man, Tony." She puts her hand on the inside of my thigh, her fingers brushing against my cojónes. She strokes lightly. I want to leap on her and take her right then, but she pulls her hand away. "I better go," she sighs. "I'm already late." She gives me a quick kiss and is gone.

I feel like I'm dancing in the clouds. Can this be really happening? Maybe Mary is some demented fantasy born out of my loneliness? Maybe I've finally gone round the bend? I don't care because she makes me feel like springtime. I pick up my trumpet and play "the red, red robin is bob, bob, bobbin' along" until my next-door neighbor, Reuben, a nonagenarian xylophone player, starts pounding on the wall.

I put away the trumpet, switch off the lights, and go to bed. Soon I'm in the limbo land between sleeping and waking. Clara and Mary are lying on either side of me; Mary has her hand delicately over my dick. Clara's head is curled on my shoulder. I hear a faint knocking at the door.

I stumble up, nearly fall, before I grab my walker and make it to the door. It's Mary. I move aside to let her in. She closes the door and puts a finger to her lips.

She pushes me back till I am sitting on the bed. She unbuttons her uniform and lets it fall to the floor. Her skin is so white she gleams in the darkness like a giant pearl. She is wearing a simple black bra and a black pair of those new-fangled thong panties. I can make out wisps of curly hair escaping the silky triangle at her vulva. This turns me on so much my pecker rises up like a periscope. Mary must sense it because quicker than I can say hallelujah, she kneels between my legs and frees my pecker from my pants. She takes it between her full lips and into her juicy mouth. She sucks gently on my cockhead as she circles my pole with her hand and starts pumping. Her movements are syncopated so as her head moves up and down on me her hand does the same. I am impressed. Mary seems to have had considerable experience.

I can feel the heat of her breasts moving on my shins. I reach down, unhook her bra, and pull it off. I lift one tit in each hand and start tracing my fingers up to the nipples and back. She seems to like this because she starts blowing me even harder. She starts tickling the little hole on the top of my cock with her tongue and miraculously I'm young again, I'm Rambo, I'm unstoppable. I start to come and come and come into her mouth like a mighty warrior. Right away, I feel embarrassed. I should have pulled out before the moment of truth. I don't know if she likes to swallow like Clara did, but then Mary downs my jism like it's good, fresh milk.

When I am drained, Mary raises herself and sits beside me, my visiting goddess. I put my arm around her. She nestles closer. "I enjoyed that," she says. "It makes me very wet." She puts her hand over me. I am still half-hard and with the touch of her palm my prick jumps up again all fine and frisky. She pulls off her panties. I pull off my pajama top, she pulls off the bottoms. She straddles me and I put my hands on her hips and help her slide up and down until we make the bedsprings sing "Begin the Beguine."

She left a little while ago. The sheet is still warm where she was lying beside me. I don't know what will happen with this surprising new romance but one thing I know for sure: right now, I'm the happiest old horndog in the world.

A TONGUE IS JUST A TONGUE

Michelle Robinson

He was sitting at the bar when Cindy and Brianna walked in. No woman who entered could help but notice him. Cindy wanted one thing and one thing only—she wanted to know what his cock tasted like. As she passed him, she noticed him noticing her, and stopped for a moment and whispered something in his ear.

"Do you know him?" Brianna asked.

"No, I've never seen him before in my life."

"Then what did you say to him?"

"I asked him if he was fantasizing about my mouth fucking his cock."

"Cindy!"

"What?"

"He's gonna be on you all night now, expecting to get some."

"There's not a thing wrong with that. I'm grown. And I want some. I haven't had a man come in my mouth since I broke up with Daniel and quite frankly, I miss it. I miss the power and intensity of making a man come.

"And as far as him following me around tonight, maybe he will and maybe he won't. If he's scared, he might not. Not all men are comfortable with a woman who's in charge of her own sexuality. It scares them. But—and this is what I'm looking forward to—if he's not scared, he'll stick around and see how far he and I can take this. And, if he does, it might very well be a helluva night of damn good sex.

"If there's one thing I've learned, it's that the five senses are the most direct link to no-holds-barred coming. In that tiny instant, I supplied him with three of the senses; sight, sound, and smell. Now all that's left are taste and touch. Most people assign sole power to the genitals and that's why so many people are underserved and dissatisfied. When I fuck a man, I fuck him with the words and sounds that roll off of my tongue, with the lingering scent of my perfume that wafts by his nostrils, the faintest brush of my fingers against his skin, my red full lips pursed with promise. The taste of my lips touching his, my tongue tasting his tongue and his tasting mine. I plan to make him come with more than just my lips or my pussy wrapped around his cock. I plan to make him come with my mind and body. I plan to march all five of his senses—and mine—out on the floor and do the dance that lovers do." And that she did.

It didn't take long for him to approach Cindy.

"Hi, I don't believe the two of us have met, at least formally. My name is Mark."

"I'm Cindy and this is my girlfriend Brianna."

Knowing full well what was soon to take place, Brianna found herself much more titillated by it all than she would've expected herself to be. She was wet between her legs and silently wished she could be as forward as her friend Cindy. As if reading her mind, Cindy suddenly broke into Brianna's thoughts.

"Mark here has never seen the view from the terrace. I told him that we would take a walk with him so that he could see it."

"We," Brianna echoed.

And with that, Cindy whispered in Brianna's ear.

"Don't be such a chickenshit. Come with us. You don't have to do anything you don't want to do, and you're free to leave whenever you like."

Before they ventured upstairs with Mark in tow, Cindy ordered a straight Coca-Cola for both her and Brianna to take with them upstairs. She knew Brianna was probably confused (under the circumstances) by why she felt the need to stop and get a plain-old Coca-Cola for them both, but she would explain to her later.

Climbing the stairs that led to the "view from the terrace," Brianna thought her heart might actually beat completely out of her chest. She couldn't remember ever having been this nervous about anything—not even when she took the bar exam for the third time.

As soon as they were upstairs, Cindy handed Brianna a glass of soda and told her to take a swig. Cindy had been drinking hers while they were climbing the staircase.

It was very cold outside and usually after mid-October or so people stopped coming up to the terrace. By this time of the year, mid-January, they were pretty much guaranteed privacy. Not that Cindy cared. There was a part of her that enjoyed the intrigue of it all; the possibility of being caught out in public with a cock inside of her mouth thrilled her immensely, and she was sure that it would have the same effect on the very hand-some young stranger standing behind her with his hard cock pressing into her back.

While Brianna stood by watching, anticipating what would

happen next, Cindy sprang into action. She turned to face Mark, whispering something in his ear.

"Are you going to feed me some of that nice hard cock of yours now, or what?" she asked.

Cindy was intent on isolating the act. Foreplay was a wonderful thing, but often the lack of foreplay could be just as big a turn-on. She wasn't going to kiss him or straddle his cock with her pussy, she was only going to suck his cock—and she was going to suck it good.

Cindy freed Mark of the pants and briefs that held his impressive member hostage and immediately wrapped her lips around him. She had taken great care to stay fully hydrated throughout the evening, and she had chewed gum and drunk plenty of fruit juice and Coca-Cola, even biting on a lemon just moments earlier. She had learned a long time ago that you couldn't give good head if you were dehydrated and even if you were, things like chewing gum, sweet drinks, and lemons went a long way to create an abundance of saliva in your mouth. She had every intention of wetting his cock completely. She planned on sliding up and down the length of his tool with the greatest of ease and with great voracity. She wanted to taste every last inch of him. Whenever she felt he wasn't wet enough, she would spit on his cock, which served two purposes: it got his cock good and wet again, but it also excited the hell out of him. The sight of her spitting on his cock, outdoors, just a few feet away from a club full of people, was almost more than he could stand. There was something so nasty and so forbidden about spitting on a man's cock—and so fucking sexy.

Every now and then Cindy would talk to Mark. She wanted all of his senses fully engaged.

"Oh, baby, you've got a beautiful fucking cock. Give me all of it."

And when she wasn't talking about his beautiful hard cock, she was talking about her girlfriend Brianna who was creeping closer and closer to where they were. Cindy could see just how excited she actually was by the way Brianna's hard nipples jutted through her black jersey-knit dress.

She knew she had made the auditory connection with him when he moaned in pleasure at her words and his cock got even harder and stiffer between her fingers. She slid her mouth up and down his cock with her hand mimicking what her mouth was doing, keeping in unison with her lips, heightening his pleasure even more, ensuring that sensation was truly optimized. Often Cindy would remove her mouth, allow the cold air to hit his cock, and slowly blow on its head with her hot breath, causing him to shiver.

By now, Cindy was happy to find that Brianna was ready for a little action herself. She had joined them and was nibbling and biting at Mark's ass, tracing his masculine glutes with her tongue, spreading the cheeks of his ass with her fingers, and slowly darting her tongue in and out of his asshole.

Cindy removed her mouth from Mark's cock just long enough to tell Brianna what she should do.

"Spit on his asshole, Bri, and then fuck his tight little asshole with your finger. Then I want you to lick his hole and his sac while I fuck his cock with my mouth. Okay?"

Brianna did exactly what her more experienced friend told her to do, as Cindy moaned in pleasure with the joy she was bringing to this cock with her mouth, looking up at Mark while she sucked him, so he was clear on just how much pleasure his tool was bringing her as well. Every now and then she would alternate between his cock and her hard nipples and go from one to the other nibbling and licking; the sounds her mouth was creating making them hotter and hotter. And the visual impact of Cindy sucking her own nipples was enough to make Mark shoot his load in her mouth, spraying the back of her throat with tremendous force. Cindy was doing her damnedest to prolong his joy (and hers) as long as humanly possible, so she had placed her thumb on that spot at the base of his cock and applied firm enough pressure to slow down the inevitable gush. Cindy knew something many don't know—the cock is not as fragile as others may make it out to be. In fact, most men enjoy the varying degrees between a firm, unyielding hand (and mouth) and a soft, supple touch.

While Brianna was licking Mark's balls, Cindy was slowly licking his shaft to the core. By the time she reached the root, both her tongue and Brianna's were inches from nirvana—and that is when Cindy began to push that exact spot, between his asshole and the root of his cock, with the flat of her tongue. She spiraled her tongue around it powerfully, covering the entire area, while Brianna plunged her tongue inside of his asshole.

His spasms were so intense, for a moment Brianna was afraid he might be having a heart attack. His body jerked and his eyes rolled back and he bellowed so loudly that it was surprising none of the club-goers below ran to see what was the matter.

Cindy was indeed an expert. What she hadn't shared with her friend Brianna was how she had truly put herself through law school. After all, there's but so much money you can make as a waitress. Cindy would have loved to share with other women her experiences as a call girl. However, she had learned through the years that not many people were as open-minded as they claimed to be. Cindy had only worked as a call girl for two years, but the data she had compiled on how to please a man was invaluable.

First, catch and release. It was a fishing term that was the key to a night of "fantabulous" sex, be it oral or otherwise.

Nothing fed fantasy and seduction quite like being caught—but not quite. When Cindy first entered the club on this particular night, she had made it crystal clear to her intended what she wanted to do to him. So, for the rest of the night, even after his initial "tenting," he was thinking of her full red lips wrapped around his cock, thereby making him as hot, horny, and ready as she was. (Sight)

Perfume in essence is designed to capture the senses. In fact, there are those—Cindy was one—who have abandoned Chanel and White Diamonds for human pheromones in an effort to more intensely promote sexual attraction. (Smell)

The taste of his own come in his mouth once Cindy had raised up and deposited it there with a passionate kiss, the mere thought of the heights of sexual freeness they had reached was enough to spring him quickly back to life as his mouth fully embraced his own emission. (Taste)

Cindy's moans of pleasure, coupled with Brianna's, heightened his awareness of his hedonistic circumstances. His own moans of delight, even the suctioning noises Cindy's mouth made on his cock, drove Mark wild. (Sound)

And, finally, the most obvious of the five—Cindy's hands never leaving his cock, Brianna's fingers exploring his tight, virgin asshole, were the final frontier that rocked him to the core. (Touch)

Without the five senses working in concert with one another, Cindy, better than anyone, knew that a tongue was just a tongue.

IT'S A WONDERFUL BLOW JOB

Simon Sheppard

I never much wanted to blow a married man. I mean, I'm sure I've done it a bunch—I'm not the most discriminating homo in the world, and when it comes to sex, men are notorious liars. But it wasn't until I met George that the "married" part of "married man" became a whole big thing.

Christmas is, as each and every one of us knows, pretty fucking stressful for a holiday that supposedly betokens peace on Earth. So what better time to hit the virtual whorehouse that is Craigslist than the Friday before Yule, right?

When he answered my ad, nearly the first thing George told me about himself was that he was wed. To a woman. I emailed back that it didn't matter to me, that I neither fetishized nor condemned men who sought out extraconnubial cock. He in turn responded that he didn't care about that, as long as I was discreet. I told him that I was, not at that point suspecting I'd write about him—but hey, I did change his name, and I won't tell you his real one, not even if you ask nicely.

George left work early so he could come by and still get back to home and hearth on time. If he was bringing home presents for the wife—and kids, if any—I was assuming he'd leave them in the car.

He had sent only the tiniest of thumbnail face shots. And, from his description, he sounded like a pretty big guy. Fine with me, but pretty big. But the truth, the awful truth, the pretty exact truth was that his looks were secondary anyway. Because I was shocked to discover that, for the honest and truly first time in my long, dissolute life, I was excited—and I mean wood-inside-the-sweatpants excited—at the prospect of having sex with a married man *precisely because he was married.* I mean, I'd always looked askance at those Craigslist ads that specified "married, bi, or straight only." Politically suspect, reeking of internalized homophobia, all that stuff. And now, suddenly, transgressively, I'd crossed over to the dark side.

Though, if he was an agent of Satan, or even an Imperial Storm Trooper, George—let's keep calling him George, shall we?—was a particularly innocuous-seeming one. When he showed up at my door, wearing a broad gold band on the fourth finger of his left hand, he was a lot cuter than his picture had led me to believe. He was also a little over half my age, weighed half again as much as me, and all that was fine.

But what was really, really, really fine was that he was cheating on his wife. With me. Sor-ry.

It turned out that George liked to deep-kiss, a delightful surprise under the circumstances, and when, during our mouth-to-mouth, I reached down, there was a hard-on, smallish but perceptible, inside his pants. Merry Christmas!

Some guys you can gradually unwrap like a, yes, Christmas present. But George backed away and stripped himself down with alacrity, buck-naked before I had a chance to unbuckle my belt.

When George's clothes are off and he's in my bed, it's clear that he's a husky boy, indeed. And that his dick is maybe five inches at most, uncut, and very, very hard, one of those intact cocks that are bright red at the business end. Kind of festive, more so if I'd done cock bondage with a green ribbon, but no matter. Since George seems neither shy nor reticent, I just go ahead and suck his dick.

Since I'm not a size queen, and my jaws get tired easily, George's little mouthful is just the right, yummy length. I give it my all: the supersuction; the tease-the-underside-with-your-tongue gambit; the nibble the foreskin game. I was born with a goodly gag reflex, though over the years, I've learned to relax, keep breathing, and deep-throat pretty sizable dicks. But in this case, I don't have to use my Advanced Cocksucking techniques to get my lips all the way down around the hairy base, which is just fine with me. I ingest the hubby's hard-on like I'm the proverbial starving man. And then I take a blow job break, lift my head above George's ample belly, and ask what the nasty part of me has been itching to ask all along. "Does your wife suck your cock?"

And George, bless him, knows just what to say, the perfect answer. "Yes, she does. But not as well as you."

"Thank you," I say, since I'm pretty damn sure it's not flattery. Yes, I'm sure that there are scads of straight women who suck cock with the same single-minded devotion, the worshipful wonder, that gay men do. I just haven't met many of them, is all I'm saying. And after all, I know what feels good to me, right, and however empathetic a woman is, unless she's a tranny, she just has to imagine the sensations of getting one's cock sucked.

I'm not being sexist here: when I've played with the unrenovated plumbing of female-to-male guys, I've pretty much had to watch for their reactions and take the rest on faith.

So I smile at George and go back south. Now, at the risk of seeming dehumanized, I have to confess that there often comes a time mid-fellatio when dick is all, and the man it's attached to becomes a matter of secondary importance, or even scorn. Maybe that's a thoroughly gay-man thing; I'd be surprised to find out that straight women patronize glory holes.

One could, if so inclined, take a vulgar Freudian view of this hunger for hard meat—proof positive that homos are developmentally stuck at a stage of immature orality. Or the queer/cock connection could be attributed, somewhat more metaphorically, to gay guys seeking to incorporate a throbbing masculinity that they deep down fear they lack. Then there's the Eucharist—but honey, we're not even going to *go* there. Which leaves us with perhaps the simplest explanation of all: gay men know that sucking dick is great.

Your choice.

One might wonder what, in an alternative universe where gay men didn't exist, the fate of the gentle art of fellatio would be. Straight men, by and large, seem to think that they're getting the best of the bargain when women give them head. We homos, on the other hand, are so enamored of cock-in-the-mouth that the roles of *top* and *bottom* become irrelevant. Who's getting what they want out of a male-on-male blow job? Well, usually both parties; the sucker (and how did *that* get to be an insult?) may justifiably feel that he's actually the one in control. I've heard it reliably reported that many a het man has to be cajoled into eating cunt. Gay men, though, have to be gagged and bound before they refrain from going down.

Did I mention that I think too much when I'm having sex?

Anyway, after another bout of pole-smoking, I decide to take my tongue even farther south. Assward ho! I rarely rim strangers anymore, but I go ahead and, lifting up his meaty thighs, plunge my tongue into his *tuchis*. I bet his wife doesn't do *that*.

I stop eating ass long enough to say, "I bet your wife doesn't do *that*." I'm really rubbing it in. Neither of us seems to mind in the least.

Well, maybe I do mind, maybe part of me minds a little. I'm the child, see, of a family where Dad unimaginatively banged his secretary on the sly. So the thought of Mrs. George sitting there back in Orinda or Mountain View or Bedford Falls or wherever, watching the blinking lights on the family Christmas tree, while I'm browning her errant hubby's ass, that makes me a tad uneasy. I guess I'm just an old-fashioned guy.

George, however, is not. After several "God, that feels good's," he lets me know that he thinks it would be a swell idea to suck my dick, too. He likes the idea, I bet, because my cock is bigger than his. Because it's mine. And—let's face it—because it's a dick.

I, in turn, like the idea because I've always found it suspect for a gay man to want nothing more than to subserviently service breeder cock…though not suspect enough, apparently, to have kept me from doing it. Still, a bit of turnabout would salve my shaft-sucking conscience. In addition, let's face it, every man, even the biggest bottom, likes his cock sucked. And—the amoral cherry on top—I'm about to get head from a verifiably married man.

I wish I could claim, for the purposes of this story, that he was virginally reluctant, had a hard time at first, but finally managed to deep-throat my dick. But either George is a cocksucking slut or a remarkably quick study, because, whoops, there it goes, my dick all the way in his mouth, on the first try.

As he's sucking away, he puts his chubby fingers on my hairy thighs, and I reach down with my right hand and stroke his wedding ring. Fuck, it *is* a wonderful life, ain't it?

Just about the time I'm wondering what would happen if George gave his wife an STD for Christmas—I mean, I'm clean, but how the hell could he be sure of that?—he takes his mouth off me and suggests it's time for me to go down on him again.

I'm not about to argue. I chew on his meaty, married tit, run my tongue over his big, married belly, and start licking his perky, married prick. I no sooner get the swollen red head between my lips, though, than George starts groaning that he's going to come. Now, I know he's got Christmas stuff to attend to—put together George Junior's trike, perhaps, or wrap Georgette's Malibu Whore Barbie—but I'm not quite ready for this to end. I take my mouth off him.

Too late. He starts gushing like a motherfucker, the whitest, thickest, creamiest goo I've seen in a long, long time. Clearly, he hasn't gotten laid at home for a while. In a split second, I figure that it's worth the risk, bob down, and catch the rest of his load in my mouth. It tastes, of course, just like gay men's cum. Only better.

Afterward—he wanted me to stand up with my cock right in his face and jack off over his chest, and I, obliging fellow that I am, did just that—we talk a bit while he's getting dressed. I tell him what a guilty pleasure it is for me to suck off a married man. He, apparently guilt-free, tells me he's glad. And he heads home to Mrs. George.

Later, after all the world's unwanted presents have been repacked and taken back to Macy's, after all the decorations have been stored away till the next Christmas season, which in recent years has started just after Halloween, I send George an email. I'm a little apprehensive; I'm hoping that blower's remorse hasn't set in and I'll have to deal with guilt pangs or, more disconcertingly, silence. But hey, it's only email, right? So, perhaps too chirpily, I tell him I'd like to do it again. He gets back to me posthaste, telling me he would, too…but then, who'd want to settle for second-rate head? More precisely, this is what he writes me: "Honestly, what I've found through doing 'this' with guys is that it really does make me feel sexy and 'desirable.' Maybe it's a midlife crisis thing, but guys call me sexy and hot even when I don't feel it myself."

I find all that sweet and somehow affirming, like I'm the Mother Teresa of illicit sex, though I'm a little baffled that someone who's only thirty-three is having a midlife crisis already. It's a nice way to rationalize cheating, though, so I don't argue. I invite him back, he accepts, but at the last minute, added work-load means he can't stop by on the way home to his wifey.

And I, ever the long-suffering other woman, email him back, "That's okay. I know we'll get together soon. Happy New Year."

DOWN ON THE BEACH

Alessia Brio

Chloe downed the remainder of her Red Stripe in one long pull and slipped away from the eclectic group gathered around the bonfire. The bass thrum of a boom box followed her up the beach, but the soporific sounds of the surf swallowed the reggae beat. The cloying aroma of hash was a bit more tenacious, though, and it carried on the humid sea-scented air—a peaceful infusion that blended the edges of her being with the coming night like smudged charcoal under an artist's thumb.

She didn't think anyone had noticed her departure, and Chloe preferred it that way. Ideally, the osmotic sensuality of a Jamaican sunset should be experienced with a lover, but airline snafus had delayed Jack's arrival. She had other options, of course, and he certainly wouldn't begrudge her an opportunity to play. Their relationship was beautiful in that way: love without limits, without the grasp and clutch of possessiveness, without smothering fear.

However, it'd been several months since they'd been together, and Chloe wanted Jack to enjoy the full force of her appetite. Determined not to mute that hunger, she distanced herself from the temptations—from the resonant vibration of the music and the enticing scent of salty, sun-kissed skin.

She dug her toes into the cool, wet sand as day surrendered to night. Deep orange tendrils spread across the horizon, fading to reds and purples until the line between sea and sky vanished. Tiny waves lapped at Chloe's ankles. Only by standing still in the crystal clear water could she feel the pull of the tide sinking her heels ever so slightly. Warmth and a peaceful passion engulfed her, smoothing her desire across her entire body so that it didn't just throb in her sex, but formed an aura that matched the silvery glow of the crescent moon on the placid surface of the sea.

Glancing over her shoulder, Chloe studied the distant cluster of bodies before unknotting her sarong. She could see them, silhouetted by the fire, but doubted they could see her. She held the soft wrap by its corners—above her head—and allowed the breeze to catch it, laughing at her whimsical impulse before letting go to watch it float softly inland and come to rest on the dry sand. Peeling off her swimsuit, she balled it up and flung it so that it landed alongside the other garment.

With arms wide, Chloe walked into the sea, submersing herself when its warmth reached her waist. It embraced her, not dousing her fire but stoking it through a symphony of sensation. It penetrated her body and her mind, and she floated on waves of want, buoyed by the desire for Jack's touch.

When the enveloping touch of the liquid began to coalesce into a pulse between her legs, she worked her way toward the shore, prolonging the need until it became integral to her existence, one with her spirit. Whole. Raw. Pure.

Although it wasn't chilly by anyone's standards, the air was cooler than the water, and Chloe's skin reacted to the change in temperature as she emerged from the water. She ran both hands through her hair, wringing as much moisture from it as possible, then shook her head in an attempt to dry it further.

That act—coupled with the effects of the beer and the pervasive arousal—made her dizzy, and she stood knee-deep in the surf with her eyes closed until the vertigo passed. Upon opening them, she discovered Jack standing on the shore, grinning at her. At first, she thought him a figment of her imagination—an apparition of desire—but then he spoke.

"You're a sight for sore eyes."

Although elated, Chloe seemed anchored where she stood, stunned and unable to move toward her lover.

"A seat opened on an earlier flight," he explained as he took off his sneakers and socks. "I got here an hour ago and have been searching rather frantically for you ever since. I suppose I should've looked first for a naked nymph in the surf." His T-shirt came off in one smooth motion and fell atop his shoes. Chloe drank in the sight of his bare chest. Shorts and boxers followed, providing an even more enticing visual buffet. A primal growl formed in the back of her throat, and she stepped forward to meet Jack as he entered the water.

He took her face in both his hands and kissed her quite tenderly—not at all what Chloe expected after such a long separation—and she resisted when he first tried to break away. Being bigger and much stronger, he easily broke her grip and held her at arm's length. For several moments, Jack looked intently into her eyes. She felt their souls reconnecting and understood then why he had slowed their collision.

"Yes," he whispered, again pulling her into his arms. "*There* you are, my love."

Chloe felt his cock grow against her tummy, and she ached to take him into her mouth. Her eyes asked—begged, really—and

Jack simply nodded. He knew exactly what she wanted. Wasting no time, she dropped to her knees. The water lapped at her bare sex, and Chloe swung one leg to the side to plant her foot in the sand—opening herself to the dance of warm, wet tongues across her clit. They fueled her arousal, but weren't strong enough to be a serious distraction.

She licked the silky head of Jack's cock, and it leapt to meet her lips in that way she so adored—like a sexual divining rod. Slipping it all the way into her mouth, Chloe buried her nose in the bristly thatch of hair at its base and inhaled deeply, murmuring her appreciation of his taste and scent.

The palms of her hands traveled up the backs of his legs, from ankles to ass, and her nails scraped the length of them on their round-trip. Jack groaned and wove the fingers of both hands through her hair, holding her head as he pushed himself even deeper into her throat. She could take everything he had to give—and take it as roughly as he wanted to give it—but Chloe wanted a different demonstration of his desire.

She savored him for a few moments before drawing back. "Huh-uh," Chloe uttered, smiling up at Jack. Taking one of his hands from her hair and directing it to the base of his cock, she continued, "*My* mouth. Y*our* hand."

With that simple directive, she returned her hands to his legs and her mouth to its home—not giving him an opportunity to object. Jack stood still, and Chloe waited patiently for him to adjust to the rules of this new game. Her tongue continued to play around his head, teasing, but she didn't move in earnest until he stroked himself—feeding her his cock.

"Mmm," Chloe purred. "Yes!" Although it was too dark for him to see the ecstasy in her expression, he could certainly hear it in the melodic sounds she made each time his hand bumped her lips.

Anyone eavesdropping would believe Chloe enjoyed the most succulent dessert and, by her own estimation, she did exactly that. With only the head of Jack's cock in her mouth, she had plenty of room to maneuver her tongue—and she kept it in constant motion. She sucked in conjunction with each of his downstrokes, milking tiny droplets of salty sweetness from his body. *Appetizers*, she'd called them very early in their relationship, and he had laughed.

Her hands cupped Jack's ass, feeling the muscles repeatedly tense and relax as the hand gripping his cock varied in speed. If he stopped, she stopped. If he slowed, she slowed. Chloe followed his lead, knowing he'd soon lose the ability to delay his orgasm. She was in no hurry to reach the end of this particular journey and, by letting Jack set their pace, she leveraged her own greed.

Their movements stirred the waters around them, making more of a disturbance than the gentle tides. Chloe's nipples brushed against Jack's thighs, sending pulses of pleasure to her clit. The guttural sounds coming from his throat told her that he'd passed that point of no return, and she moved one of her hands from his ass to her clit—hoping to join him when he came and knowing it wouldn't take much of an effort.

"Babe, that's so...so sexy," Jack growled. "Touch yourself for me while I...I..." His words were lost to the night as his come pulsed into her throat. Chloe pinched her clit—hard—and shuddered as her own orgasm blossomed. Together they sang a syncopated song of exclamations and endearments.

Jack pulled Chloe to her feet. Her knee—the one on which she'd been balancing—buckled in protest, and he steadied her. Looking intently into her eyes again, he smiled. "*There* you are, my love."

GETTING USED TO IT

Tenille Brown

Herbert Miller simply couldn't get used to it, which was why, even after three years, the stark smell of his wife Evelyn's attempt at baking brisket still made him wrinkle up his nose. And why, when she asked him how he liked it, he just nodded while he chewed and attempted to swallow.

One would think by now that he *would* have gotten used to it, like he had that irritating lemon pine stuff she used to clean the bathroom that always burned his nose. But the scent of the meat sent him reeling, and every time she began cooking it, Herbert would sit in his chair, read his paper, and hope that there would be a kink in the stove, or that Evelyn would be a little heavy with the seasoning and the beef would, for once, be edible.

But, on a lazy Sunday afternoon as Herbert sat across from his wife sawing into the dry hunk of beef, he knew that, once again, he had been disappointed.

"So, how is it?" Evelyn asked.

She had waited until his mouth was full of the stuff, and she leaned forward, her elbows on the table, her soft, brown eyes hopeful.

It was a question Herbert knew would come, and he also knew that what he would offer in return would be a nod and a wink.

It threw her off course and made her giddy, like she had done something special, and in a way she had. Herbert had learned long ago that it took a very special talent to ruin an otherwise damned good brisket.

But Herbert never held it against her. It was only one meal, after all, and she only prepared it every now and then. There wasn't any reason to go and hurt her feelings when there were so many other things she cooked so well.

Like her pot roast, for instance. It was the best he had ever tasted, and he told her so every time she made it. But when it came to the brisket, he had decided that saying nothing was easier. So, today, he cut it up into small bites and pushed it around on his plate. He ate all of his cabbage and most of his rice and when Evelyn wasn't looking, he slipped into the kitchen and scraped the uneaten brisket into the trash, no harm, no foul.

And just to get his mind off of it, Herbert playfully patted his wife on the ass and invited her to bed early. *He* would do the dishes, he told her; and the leftover brisket, he would take care of that as well, just she wait and see.

Herbert knocked on Minnie Williams's front door, anxiously sliding his foot across the straw welcome mat. It was one of those new things everyone was plopping down at their door, and he was sure it would have been something for Evelyn to carry on and on with Minnie about. He didn't know why she couldn't have come over here herself.

But Evelyn was always getting him to do her dirty work. This time it was picking up a dish that she had sent some peach cobbler in when Minnie was under the weather last week. Herbert chuckled to himself because she had contemplated sending brisket, and he himself had saved Minnie from it.

Minnie came to the door then, apron around her plump waist, hair every which way. Typical Minnie.

"Hey, Herbert. Come on in and let me get you Evelyn's dish." She was drying her hands with a dish towel and smiling, out of breath from the simple walk to the front door.

Herbert shook his head. "That's quite all right. I can just wait right here 'til you bring it out."

Minnie shrugged. "That's fine, too. Whatever suits you."

Then Minnie left the door cracked, and the scent hit Herbert like a sucker punch that knocked him clear off his feet.

He poked his head inside, sniffing. "I do apologize for disturbing your dinner."

Herbert heard Minnie suck her teeth. "Don't be silly. There's nobody here to enjoy it but me. I'm just finishing up a little old brisket in the oven."

"Brisket?" Herbert asked, as if he hadn't known. As if the smell of it didn't have him swooning right there on her front step.

"Yeah, it was on sale and I had a taste for it, so I said, hell, why not? Why, you want a taste?"

Herbert was sure his body had made it inside the door before his mouth formed the words, "Yes, please," and before he knew it, he was sitting at Minnie's kitchen table, napkin spread over his lap, hefty plate of brisket and cabbage in front of him.

"I tell you, Minnie, this is some of the best brisket I've ever had in my mouth," Herbert said between mouthfuls. The more truthful thing to say might have been that it was *the* best, but Herbert thought it best to tone it down a little, lest he disrespect his wife, his mother, hell, every bogus brisket he had ever tasted.

Minnie nodded, pleased at the compliment. "Well, then, why don't you take a plate home? I've got plenty here."

Herbert briefly considered it. The pure goodness of the meal had made him drunk. But he quickly came to his senses.

"No, no, I couldn't do that."

Minnie rubbed her hands on her apron and took Herbert's plate away. "I suppose you're right."

Herbert knew that Minnie understood. She knew that he might just as well slap Evelyn in the face as bring a plate of another woman's food into her house.

So she offered him a glass of tea, but he turned that down, too.

Herbert didn't want to chase the meal with anything, didn't want anything to water down the taste that he would surely savor the whole way home.

The scent invaded his nostrils long after he had left Minnie's house, and when he got home, he brushed his teeth for four minutes instead of the usual two. And even after he rinsed twice and sucked on a peppermint, he still worried that another woman's brisket lingered on his breath.

So that night, when Evelyn crawled up next to him, he kissed her quickly on the forehead, rubbed her on the back, and slept with his back turned.

Herbert would never get used to it, not ever. It was the odd feeling of Evelyn's mouth on his cock, the same as the first time she had done it, and still as dissatisfying. It was what Herbert called *special attention*, the act of Evelyn taking him hurriedly into her mouth and pulling him in like a wet vacuum, but Herbert wouldn't have minded if Evelyn paid no attention at all.

It didn't happen often, but every now and then she got the urge, like this particular Friday night after she got lucky at bingo and treated two of her girlfriends to wine spritzers. She came home a little frisky, with a lopsided grin on her face.

Herbert felt a tightening in his chest when Evelyn crawled onto the bed and crouched just above his groin. As usual, she completely ignored his balls. She took too much of him into her mouth at once and had to retreat. On her second attempt, she pulled too hard and, as much as he adjusted and guided his hips, her teeth still made sharp contact with his cock.

Evelyn whispered an apology and Herbert lay there biting his lip, his eyes squeezed shut, pretending she was doing a fantastic job. He supposed that, for some, this might be something to bring up in casual conversation, or even during heated arguments over who was or wasn't doing what to satisfy whom, but it wasn't a usual occurrence in their bedroom, not like her riding him like a stallion, or her clawing at his back when he was on top of her. He thought the matter better left where it was, undisclosed.

So when Evelyn's eyes made contact with his and she received the smile and nod of reassurance, she lowered her moist crotch onto his waiting cock and did what she did best, riding Herbert until he came.

"Even your leftovers are good, Minnie."

Herbert leaned over a plate of them one Wednesday evening while Evelyn was at her sister's. In fact, he looked at the plate of reheated brisket and cabbage as opposed to looking at Minnie.

She wasn't a beautiful woman. She was a little rough around the edges for his taste and was too loud most times. But, he noticed on this certain Wednesday, she had the most perfect set of teeth he had ever seen. And her lips—he hadn't paid attention to her lips before, how plump and moist they were, how she licked them when she was nervous.

Herbert noticed that Minnie was nervous now, watching him eat his second helping of brisket and cabbage. Her lips were glossy and full and today, sipping on a tall Bloody Mary in the middle of the afternoon, they were a little loose.

"You know, Herbert," she said. "You're a real good man. You're respectful...and nice enough not to let your wife know that she can't cook brisket worth shit."

Herbert stiffened in his chair.

Minnie saw the tension. "Oh, relax, man. I was just making fun. Hell, every ham I get my hand on turns out dry as a chip. So, we're not all perfect. Matter of fact, is there anything else she's not good at 'cause I've got a fridge full of leftovers?"

Herbert thought for a moment and said, "Well, no, everything else, she does pretty good at." He sheepishly added, "Cooking-wise, I mean."

He wasn't sure how Minnie had taken that, but she said, "Well, then, is there anything else I can do for you?"

And for the briefest moment, Herbert thought about telling Minnie, thought about asking her if there was anything else that *she* was good at.

And, as though he had given voice to his thoughts, Minnie approached him, with more sway in her hips than before. Her eyes hung lower, her lips were a little poutier. She leaned over, and, as bold as ever, planted a soft, wet kiss on his neck.

Herbert nearly jumped out of his chair. "Minnie!"

She clutched her chest. "Oh, my. Damn, Herbert, I read you all wrong, didn't I?"

"Yes, Minnie, you did. All wrong. Completely wrong."

"Well, you'll have to excuse me for being so forward, but I just figured since you've been coming here so regularly, sitting at my table, cleaning your plate, I thought that maybe you were interested in a little more than brisket." Minnie's hands were defiantly on her hips.

Herbert found himself at a crossroads. And, after thinking for just a moment, he decided the direction he would take.

He took Minnie's hands in his own and held them in his lap. He looked directly into her eyes as he guided her hands up toward his crotch. Instinctively, she rubbed, and soon he was hard and begging to be free.

Minnie's eyes stayed on his as she took a final sip of her drink, asking if it was okay, if she was going too far. Herbert gasped his approval when she unzipped his trousers and pulled his erect cock from his boxers. He trembled when her soft, bare hand touched him there. She held him with as much tenderness as she did aggression. She was altogether gentle and vicious, touching and massaging until he was sure he would burst out of his skin.

Finally, Minnie got down on her knees, her cotton dress fanned out around her, and took Herbert into her mouth. She didn't take in more than was necessary, and she didn't neglect any part of him.

The inside of her mouth was hot, the attention from her tongue tingly and spicy. She glided up and down Herbert's cock with ease, her soft, full lips occasionally making contact with his shaft.

Minnie used her warm tongue to trace a path along the length of him. She curled her lips around the head of his cock and planted gentle kisses.

Minnie didn't waver when Herbert began to rock in his seat, when he began to tremble against her lips. She remained still when Herbert growled deep in his throat and came forcefully inside her mouth.

In fact, Minnie smiled, traces of Herbert's passion glossing her lips.

She stood up and straightened her dress. She took Herbert's plate from the table and, as if she had done nothing at all, said, "You come back for more anytime, all right?"

Herbert nodded, straightened up his pants, and left Minnie's house. And at home he gave his well-worn cock several vigorous swipes of a hot washcloth. But still, he worried that his wife would crouch between his legs and find traces of Minnie's lipstick. Next time, he would be sure to ask her to wipe it off first.

Yes, next time.

Herbert was always thinking of the next time, and he had become quite comfortable with the regularity of the meetings between him and Minnie, eating her brisket, feeling the warmth of her mouth on him.

It had gotten so that Evelyn's brisket was absolutely intolerable. It was drier every time it landed on his plate, tougher every time he attempted to saw into it. And maybe it was just him, but Herbert swore that Evelyn had taken a new and sudden interest in his cock. She was more apt to kiss it now, and he swore each time she was more careless with her teeth, more aggressive with her mouth. Each time he wished she wouldn't bother at all.

But Herbert fought through it, living for the afternoons he would steal away to Minnie's. Herbert had talked himself into not turning in that direction today, and now he fumbled with his keys, even sticking the wrong one in the door. It was something he didn't normally do, because even in the dark, he was used to his front lock. But perhaps it was the new straw welcome mat that distracted him, or the scent of berries lingering around the windows as opposed to lemon, or perhaps it was the scent of pot roast that met Herbert abruptly at the front door.

"You okay in here, Evelyn?" he asked, almost afraid to come inside. He supposed there wasn't any real way to not sound concerned.

Evelyn peeked out from the kitchen and said, "I'm fine. Why?"

Herbert walked in and nodded toward the covered steaming dish on the stove.

"Oh, that!" Evelyn's hand went up to her neck and fumbled with the collar of her shirt. "Pot roast, yes. Damned brisket went up another dollar and a half a pound, can you believe it?"

"That *is* crazy. Damned meat market. Always finding ways to get in your pockets."

Evelyn nodded her agreement. "And you know, Herb, I had enough money in my purse to get *three* briskets, but I'll be damned if I'll pay three ninety-nine a pound for something I just paid a dollar seventy-nine for two weeks ago. Highway robbery is what it is."

Herbert fought to contain his grin. He nodded simply and said, "Yep. Couldn't agree with you more."

"But I guess that Minnie Williams just doesn't have that way of thinking. She just threw one in her basket without even looking at the price. It was a big one, too, for just her. She must be expecting company or something."

"Must be." Herbert hoped he sounded unaffected.

"Hear she's been having company pretty regularly, lately. Know anything about it?" Evelyn asked this without even looking at him, she just set a plate aside and served Herbert a large piece of roast beef.

Herbert shook his head. "That's news to me."

He looked away from his wife as he immediately began cutting in to the delicate piece of meat. He tore into it right there at the kitchen counter.

Evelyn leaned against the counter with her arms folded.

"So, I did pretty good, then?"

Herbert leaned over and kissed his wife, his lips still greasy from the roast. "Baby, you did great. And you know, it wouldn't bother me even a little if you never brought another brisket into this house."

Evelyn's eyes narrowed with the sharp realization of what Herbert was actually saying, and for a moment he was afraid he had hurt her feelings, but she stepped closer to him, returned his kiss and said, "That would be fine by me. Brisket's never been my thing anyway."

And Herbert supposed he could have left it at that, let things be—but as good as the pot roast had tasted, as tender as the moment had become between him and his wife, Herbert still found himself craving something else.

So, after an hour and a half of sipping lemonade and reading the paper, he decided to get seconds. He got up and put his hat on his head, muttered something to Evelyn about some business with George Stanley, and hurried out the door.

Burned meat was the aroma that filled Minnie Williams's house when she opened the front door, fanning at a black cloud of smoke.

"I don't know what the hell happened, Herbert," she said, clearing her throat. "I lay down to take a nap while the meat was cooking, but that's what I always do. Never in all my natural life have I ever burned a brisket."

Herbert leaned back on his heels and whistled.

"It's just that the cut was so big this week, and I'm usually pretty good at timing it, but I guess I was off. And crazy me, I slept so hard back there I damn near burned myself up!"

Herbert searched for something to say, but all that crossed his lips was, "Damn, Minnie, that's something."

"Yeah. Hope you weren't too hungry."

Herbert shook his head, absentmindedly taking steps back from her front door. "Matter of fact, I just ate not too long ago, and I'm pretty damned full from Evelyn's pot roast. In fact, I don't know why I even came over here."

Minnie's voice suddenly became throaty, seductive. "I'll bet you *I* know why you came over. And I'll bet you I know what can take your mind off that burned brisket in there."

Minnie stepped to the side and let Herbert come in. She led him to her bedroom and shut the door. She guided him toward her queen-sized bed and eased him down. Then Minnie got down on her knees.

And for a moment, Herbert *did* forget that Minnie's kitchen smelled like a burned forest. For a while he *did* forget that Minnie had ruined one fine piece of meat.

Herbert guessed that this strange feeling was what distracted him for a while, kept him from noticing that what Minnie was doing to his cock was nothing short of awkward and disjointed.

Herbert backed away.

Minnie looked up at him, dumbfounded. "Something the matter, Herb?"

"Yeah, you just…it felt…You feel different, Minnie."

She was thoughtful for a moment, then Minnie began to nod slowly. "Oh, yeah. I suppose it could be those two teeth I got pulled last week. They were aching like a son-of-a-bitch. Don't worry, though, baby, you'll get used to it."

And Herbert could have told Minnie, let her know that he didn't get used to things, but a stubborn old bird like Minnie Williams would never believe it.

So, Herbert gently guided Minnie's head away from his crotch.

"What's wrong? You don't want to at least give it a try?"

Herbert shook his head. "Nah, Minnie. In fact, I need to be getting on home. Got some leftovers I want to get my hands on before Evelyn hoops 'em out the back door."

And he slipped out as easily as he had slipped in, his stomach already rumbling.

And it was much later, after falling asleep in his chair with a full belly, that Herbert felt something new just below his waist, something cool and sweet on his exposed cock.

"Evelyn!" Herbert bolted upright in his chair.

The sudden call of her name made Evelyn jump.

"What, Herbert? You trying to scare the hell out of me?"

Herbert adjusted himself in his chair. "No, I just...Well you just...surprised me, that's all."

And Evelyn grinned. "Well, that was the point. You just looked so fine lying there napping, and you got to sleeping so deep you didn't even notice that you had..."

Herbert saw Evelyn struggling to find the words. Then he looked down at his groin. Like a man in his prime, he had gotten hard in his sleep.

"Oh. Okay." He was almost embarrassed.

Evelyn continued. "And well, I thought it might be nice for you to wake up to something special."

It was then that Herbert realized it. It had been nice. It had been good. It had been *exciting*. Herbert looked down at his crotch.

He was still hard!

"Well, you were right, Evelyn, it *was* quite nice and...different. What did you do?"

Evelyn cocked her head. "Different...different...Nothing, I don't think." Then she smiled with the realization. "Oh, right. I guess it could be that peppermint I dropped in my tea. I had a bit of a scratchy throat. You liked it?"

But instead of saying the words, Herbert reached for Evelyn's shoulders and guided her back to his crotch. He shifted himself into comfort and leaned back as his wife lowered her mouth back onto his cock.

And as she blew cool breaths on his naked skin, as her minty tongue worked its way around him, he counted in his head how many peppermints were left in the bag on their nightstand.

And it felt good. It felt new. It felt like something that Herbert could maybe even get used to.

COCKSUCKER

Lori Selke

He asks if he can suck my dick.

I'm still donning the harness, cinching the straps around my thighs tight. There is nothing elegant about this process. The transition from just me to "chick with dick" is a sensitive one. I always want to hide in the bathroom until it's over. But tonight, I left the door ajar, and there he is, standing in the doorway. I can see him in the mirror. He looks a little shy right now, which is reassuring.

Strapping it on for my man is one thing. I love men who are in touch with their asses, who aren't embarrassed by the plea-sure they get when I stick my fingertip in their anuses while I'm giving them head, who have learned to ask for that, and more. I like anal sex, too, I know how good it can feel when it's done right, and I'm glad to share that with them. Men who aren't so focused on their dicks are better lovers, in my experience. And it's nice to be able to give instead of take, to turn the tables once in a while.

But this isn't *Deep Throat*. He doesn't have a clit in his larynx. I don't quite get it. Of course I know that it makes as much sense as me wanting to suck his cock. Except that I get off on the fact that I can concentrate so clearly on his pleasure. I know he feels each stroke of my tongue, because I can see him react. He won't get that kind of feedback from what's hanging between my legs right now. But I can tell that it's taken a lot for him to even ask this of me. Normally, if he wants to try something new, he just plunges ahead. This man is no Sensitive New Age type, always checking and double-checking everything out of "respect." I hate that. Those guys are the most unbelievably boring in bed. I think that a lot of them have secret kinky fantasies about being taken and used by some leather-clad dominatrix type, but they're too cheap to just go see a pro.

I turn around. My little purple dildo is bobbing between my legs.

"Okay," I say. "Get down on your knees."

He scrambles to the floor, but doesn't move any closer to me or my dick.

"We can do this, but on one condition," I say.

He nods.

"Tell me why."

He swallows once, then licks his lips nervously. The sight makes me just a little bit wet. I am obsessed with his mouth. I have been since the day we met. He has a big mouth, both literally and figuratively. He loves to talk. He loves to kiss me. I bought concealer for the very first time ever after our third date, when he left a few hickies a little too high on my neck.

I love to bite his lip and listen to him gasp. I love to listen to the sounds he makes when he's close to coming. Whenever I hear him moan, I want to press my fingers against that mouth and feel the vibrations those soft sounds make.

I didn't think my question would be so hard to answer. But I can see the bulge in his jeans.

"It's a turn-on," I prompt. "Why?"

"Because it's wrong."

I raise an eyebrow and wait for him to continue.

"It's dirty. It's something I'm not supposed to do."

"It's dirty?" I ask.

"Yes," he says, and I can tell by the huskiness in his throat that he means it. "It's nasty. A girl isn't supposed to have a cock. She isn't supposed to get turned on watching me suck it. But baby, I can tell you'd get turned on. You like to watch me, and I want to do it for you."

I take a step toward him. One more step, and my little purple dick will be right in his face.

"Go on," I say.

"There isn't much else to it," he says. "I love the way you look, standing over me. I love having you inside me."

One more step. His mouth opens.

"Slow," I say. "Go slow. I want to see it. I want to see everything."

And he does. His big mouth and my little dick he could probably swallow it all in one gulp but instead, he works it delicately, his tongue darting in and out of his mouth, wetting his lips, sweeping the ridge of the cockhead over and over again. Even though I can't feel a thing, he's teasing me, building up my anticipation. Putting on a show.

I wish it were more than just a show. I don't have penis envy, not really. That's not it. I want his desire to give me pleasure, to be sincere and direct. No performing. Deeper than that.

I want him to touch me. I lean over and whisper in his ear, "Do you know how wet you're getting me?"

He shakes his head, swallowing my dildo deeper. I put my

hand on the back of his head and hold him there, then pull my hips back slowly. "I think you should check," I say with a smile, and lift his hand to my pussy, which is dripping. Then I clamp his hand between my thighs and start to fuck his mouth.

He's right, this is nasty and dirty and entirely wrong, and it's getting me off, too.

He wants to finger me, to make me come while I am in his mouth. And I'd like that. After a while, I let his hand go and spread my legs. The orgasm he gives me comes fast and hard. I can't help but snap my hips forward, twice, three times, filling his mouth with my cock. He's jacking himself off beneath me. I don't think I'm going to get in his ass tonight after all.

A few days later, we are in bed. I am just about asleep when he whispers in my ear, "I have another fantasy."

I make a small noise to indicate I am listening, even though I am so tired it takes an effort to concentrate on his words.

"I want someone to come in my mouth."

"I've come in your mouth lots of times," I mumble. "You want me to sit on your face, just ask."

"That's not what I meant." I hear him shifting behind me. He drapes an arm over my hip and buries his face in my shoulder. By the time he speaks again, I have to drag myself back from the lip of unconsciousness to listen.

"I want a boy to come in my mouth. A guy. Another man."

I'm not sure if I should say anything or not. I am almost afraid to move. I am suddenly wide awake.

"And I want you to watch," he continues.

Is this his way of coming out to me? Is my boyfriend bisexual?

Does it matter right now?

I can feel how tense he is against me. He's afraid. This is a fragile moment. If I say the wrong thing, he will close down, maybe forever. I resist the urge to make light of his confession, to say something flippant.

"Do you have anyone in mind?" I ask after a moment.

"Not really," he says. And I can feel some of my own muscles uncurl.

I uncurl a little too much, and before I can stop it, it slips out of my mouth. "My dick wasn't enough for you?" I can hear the lightness in my tone, but what if he misunderstands?

"It's different," he says, and then stops. If I want any more from him now, I'm going to have to do the work.

So I ask, "Why do you want me to watch?"

He sighs and runs his fingers through my hair. "If you're there, it feels safe," he says.

"Safe like you'll know I'm not jealous?"

"No. Safe like I know you'll watch out for me."

I want to laugh, to scoff, to say, "You're afraid of a little cock? They're such fragile things, there's nothing at all to be scared of. Look, I let yours inside me as often as I can get it. If I can do that and like it, why do you need me to hold your hand when you try it out?"

I want to say, "I never expected you to be such a timid little virgin."

I want to say, "I don't think that's safe."

I want to ask, "Do you check out the tackle of the other guys at your gym? Have you picked one out? Do you jerk off to the thought of your mouth on his cock?"

I want to ask, "Have you been thinking about him while we fuck?"

I want to ask, "Am I just a substitute for what you really crave?"

And some of those questions I might just ask some other day.

But I know better than to ask them right now.

So instead I say, "That sounds pretty hot." And I realize, after I say it, that it's true.

I also realize that his cock is hard against the small of my back. So I shift a little, until I've half-turned to face him, and I've opened my legs to let him slide between my thighs. I can't see his face; it's too dark. But I look at him anyway, imagine looking into his eyes, imagine looking into his eyes while he sucks off another man.

I'm wet enough now that it's easy for him to enter me. We start out slow, but it doesn't last long. I come hard, and he comes right after me. His moans are high and full of relief. So are mine.

PREGO

Alison Tyler

We have such a fucked-up, twisted, we'll always have (*Last Tango in*) Paris sort of relationship, that nothing fazes me anymore. I mean, nothing in the bedroom. Even our most vanilla activities tend to involve accoutrements such as rubber dishwashing gloves, velvet blindfolds, and Wesson oil. So I suppose I shouldn't have found it odd at all to walk through the swinging doors of our kitchen and discover Jackson fucking the jar of spaghetti sauce.

But I did.

Both find him, and find it odd.

On any other night, I would have seen him fucking that wide-mouthed jar, and thought, *Yum. Dinner.* I might have taken a seat at the counter and watched, or even have asked him why he'd chosen Prego rather than Ragu. I can imagine wondering idly whether Garden Variety worked better for fucking than Marinara. But we were currently hosting a dinner party for six, and I could see from the open cabinet that he was using our last jar.

"Please, Carrie," he said when he heard me enter.

With the very real knowledge of our invited guests waiting in the dining room, and the equally real vision of my husband fucking a jar of pasta sauce, all my thoughts came to a basil-fragranced stop.

"Please," he said again, his voice as hungry as I imagined our guests to be.

Please what? I wondered. *Please slip out to the grocery store and buy more sauce. Please go and tell our friends that dinner's going to be late. Please...*

"Get down on your knees," he continued.

I was still in mild shock. Jackson had on a pair of black slacks and a black fitted T-shirt. He looked dashing and normal, except for the fact that he was holding a jar of pasta sauce at waist level. Water for the angel hair bubbled rapidly behind him on the stove. The sauce was the last thing, the most pressing thing, left to cook.

How *could* he have...why *would* he have?

"On your knees," he said, and now there was no *scusi* in his voice, no *per favore* to his tone. I watched the way he was dipping his cock into the half-full bottle, and for a moment I forgot all about our guests. Forgot that we'd decided to host a dinner party in honor of our tenth anniversary. Forgot that sauce stains.

I dropped to my knees on the slick linoleum floor and waited. Usually, I know what I'm doing in this situation. On my knees, mouth open, Jackson's cock slipping back and forth past my parted lips. The warm wet heat of my mouth enveloping him. But now, now what did he want from me? He had the pasta jar; he didn't need my mouth, too, did he, greedy thing?

Apparently, he did.

"Taste this," he said, smiling that sly Jackson smile at me, "and tell me what you think it needs."

I looked at his cock, all covered in pasta sauce, and then I looked back up at him.

"Are you serious?"

I shouldn't have asked. He pushed forward, grabbing the back of my hair at the same time, and suddenly, I found myself sucking Prego from his rock-hard shaft. I should say that I am a pasta junkie. I don't care if pasta is the cheapest thing for a restaurant to make, don't give a damn if nineteen dollars for a plate of macaroni is obscene. Every time we go out, that's what I order. I like red sauce best, what Italians mean when they say gravy.

And I should also say that I love sucking cock. I have gotten on my knees for Jackson in far stranger places than our kitchen. I've sucked him on the ferry from Larkspur to San Francisco, with the salt spray behind me and San Quentin to my left. I've drained him on an airplane, the red-eye from LAX to LaGuardia, while our fellow passengers snoozed zombielike beneath those thin gray throwaway blankets, and I worked hard to keep my slurping sounds to a minimum. And I've sucked him on our fire escape, overlooking Chestnut Street, as early morning commuters slogged toward yet another workday.

But I had never mixed these two pleasures before—sauce and sucking, fellatio and food. Not until now. Not until Jackson had finished slamming that bottle of sauce to death, and was ready for me to clean up every wayward drop.

For only a moment did I worry about what the sauce would do to my face, my hair, my outfit. For only one sliver of time did I hesitate, remembering my best friend and her fiancé out there in the dining room, talking about the Oscars with Jackson's college roommate, Eli, and his lover, Joe. What would they think if one were to push through our swinging kitchen door and find me on my knees, covered in sauce?

"Oh, *prego*," Jackson murmured, and I had to fight off the giggles that threatened to spill out. We'd gone on our honeymoon to Italy. We'd learned all of five words during the two weeks we were there: *grazie, per favore, scusi*, and *prego*. We'd said the words constantly to each other, pretending we were having legitimate conversations, like the other couples in the cafés.

Grazie, grazie.

Per favore.

We'd spoken those phrases to each other in bed, Jackson stroking me; sweetly touching my hair, my face; then flipping me onto the mattress, spitting on his palm and oiling up his cock. Saying, "*Per favore*, Carrie," before thrusting inside of me, sealing himself to me.

During our honeymoon, I hadn't worried that he was the last man I'd ever fuck. Instead, I'd thought with pleasure that we would be fucking together forever. Just the two of us. In our twisted, kinky, we'll always have Milan and Venice and Rome sort of ways. And now we were adding to the repertoire, my mouth working hungrily on Jackson's sauce-covered cock, my pussy twitching in anticipation of what might be next on the menu. When I cleaned off the sauce, would he bend me over our island and screw me? Or would he spread me out on our Corian countertop and drizzle olive oil all over my skin?

But maybe, I decided, I shouldn't worry so much about *secondo* when we were still on the appetizer. I could feel the cool black-and-white linoleum through my fishnets. I was infinitely aware of the flavor of the sauce in my mouth, combined with the real scent of Jackson's cock, Jackson's skin.

My tongue flicked out to touch his balls as I brought one hand into play. I wrapped my fist around the base of his shaft

as I continued to bob on the head. What had made him dip his
cock into the sauce in the first place? I wondered. What had
gone through his mind as he'd unscrewed the lid of the wide-
mouthed jar?

Unfortunately, I couldn't ask. My mouth was too busy, too
full. I could feel the sauce on my cheeks now, could feel the
spread of it from my lips to my chin.

He was groaning softly as I sucked him, and he pushed my
hair off my forehead and gazed down at me. I wondered if sauce
had splattered my dress. If my breasts, visible in the V-neck of
my scarlet jersey, were freckled with the juicy tomato puree.

I continued to suck him even after all the sauce was gone, so
that his cock was clean and shiny from the wetness of my mouth.
Jackson tried to lift me up then, and I guessed he was going to
fuck me, but I couldn't let him. The sensation was so sweet,
sucking him to the sounds of clinking glasses in the dining room,
to the knowledge that at any moment we might be discovered. I
could see the half-filled bottle of Prego on the counter, and that
turned me on more than anything I could have imagined. Who
would ever have guessed—forget oysters or ginger—this pasta
sauce was an aphrodisiac? Thinking of Jackson just screwing
that jar while the rest of us waited for our pasta course made
me wetter than I could have imagined. I fantasized about all of
the actions he'd been doing while I had busily entertained our
guests—envisioned him undoing his slacks and slipping his cock
into the sauce-filled jar. The sound must have been intense. That
sucking sound.

Oh, fuck.

I put one hand between my legs then, touching myself
through the layer of my dress and the creamy white panties
I had on beneath. I could sense right when Jackson had
reached his limits, because first I tasted the salty flavor of his

precome, and then the liquid of his climax filled my mouth.

Practice has made me an expert at swallowing him down, at draining his cock without spilling a drop. I felt pleased with myself as I backed up to give him room, but my fingers didn't stop their spirals over my clit.

"Show me," Jackson begged. "*Per favore.*"

Grinning like a fool, I lifted my dress, still kneeling on the floor. Jackson got on the floor with me, and his fingers took over. I looked down to see the red stain of the sauce from his fingertips mark my panties. How sexy was that? I couldn't stop staring as he rotated his fingertips right over the placket of my panties. I have always loved being touched through a barrier, and this time was no different. Except, in a way, it was. Because there was sweet sauce on his hands, so that I could see the trail of his touches, see the path his fingers took. I wanted that sauce all over me, wanted him to mark me with the tomato puree. Then suddenly I was coming, his middle finger hitting my clit in the perfect rhythm. I clutched on to him, aware that we both smelled like basil and oregano, aware that the pasta water was rollicking now. That we had nothing to serve our guests.

My eyes were glazed when Jackson stood. I watched him, but I didn't understand. He moved me to the far doorway, not the one leading to our dining room, but the one that led out to the hall. Moved me so that I was far away from him, and then, before I could say a word, he dropped the sauce jar so that it shattered on the floor.

"What?" I stammered. "Why?"

"What do you think?"

The remaining sauce went everywhere. The breaking of the bottle served to give us both a reason to change—to apologize to our guests for the slight delay in their meal, to head to the bathroom down the hall for a quick cleanup.

And a quicker fuck.

Jackson took me for real in the bathroom, took me against the shower, the scent of soap washing away the last remnants of the Prego. I was sad to see the water turn from red to clear, I must admit. And I think Jackson felt the same way. As we dried off together, I saw him lick the last drop of sauce from his top lip.

"Delicious," he told me. "We'll have to cook for guests more often."

When we returned, Eli was in the kitchen, whipping up a sauce from frozen pesto. He and Joe had taken it upon themselves to clean up, and Joe was gingerly sweeping the shards of the bottle into our dustpan.

"*Grazie, grazie,*" Jackson said with his usual buoyant charm.

"*Prego,*" Eli replied easily as he stirred the pot on the stove.

I felt my cheeks turn as red as the sauce, still clinging to the shards of broken glass.

EQUANIMITY UNBOUND

Craig J. Sorensen

Jess had knocked me more than once on it. "Brandon, you're just too uptight."

True, I didn't own a single pair of jeans. Even my jogging outfits were too crisp to be really comfortable. Damn it, I'd tried to loosen up, but it just never worked out. I don't think that this was ultimately what broke us up, but I'm sure it didn't help.

So there I was at the mall on a Tuesday evening, and I'd just finished an Italian ice at a small stand near the men's store where they'd had a "buy one, get one half-price" sale on Arrow shirts. I toted my bag of button-down, pale long-sleeved shirts toward the garbage can to toss the empty cherry ice cup away. My eyes settled on a store I'd passed a hundred times.

Inside teenagers and twentysomethings pored over T-shirts and ball caps with salacious messages emblazoned on them. In the back, lava lamps and neon lights glowed. Glasses, cups, and clocks extolled the praises of Guinness ale and Corona beer. My hand lingered over the opening to the trash. I drew a long breath of the incense-tinted air wafting from the store. Maybe a nice T-shirt would be a good way to effect the dilating of my clenched butt. The journey of a thousand miles and all that. The cup fell with a hollow thwack.

I walked inside and felt all eyes upon me. They probably weren't, but I felt them all the same. I was the only man in a double-breasted pin-striped suit in the place. I did my best to act casual.

"Findin' everything okay, babe?"

I turned to the voice. A short young woman with a goth pallor and bold black tribal tattoos extending out from her tight T-shirt smiled. The words AVENGED SEVENFOLD and a skull with bat wings adorned the T-shirt. I didn't know what an Avenged Sevenfold was, but my eyes lingered on the sprawled bat wings on her chest. Actually they settled on the thick nipples that pointed from tightly outlined small breasts. I lifted my glance apologetically to her eyes. "Uh—yeah—I'm fine."

She winked as the chipped black fingernails of her left hand combed through her spiked purple hair. She had a post through the middle of her black lower lip that accentuated the crease of a natural pout. "Lemme know if you need anything." She turned to a group of three looking through the large rack of posters.

"Analisse? How you been?" one of the customers said to the salesgirl. They hugged remotely. "I'm surprised to see you still here. Haven't you graduated college?"

"Yeah, I'm in grad school."

I couldn't help but snap my head toward Analisse. Her pale gray eyes, just a shade or two darker from the bright whites around them, locked briefly with mine. She returned to her conversation.

"God, who'da thunk it, girl? You? In grad school?" Her surprise would have been insulting to me.

Analisse just shrugged dispassionately. "It's no big thing, Carla."

I recalled how I had been a classic underachiever in high school. *If only Brandon would apply himself.* Looking at my mediocre marks at the end of my first semester of college it occurred to me: it was all up to me now. Mom and Dad weren't there to please, and they weren't there to rebel against. I went from a solid 2.0 to the Dean's List in one motion. It seemed so simple, a brief defining moment, looking back on it. But now my heart pounded at the memory of the violent inner struggle.

Carla continued extolling her old friend with praises. It was obvious that this was wearing on the tattooed woman. I waved. "Excuse me, miss?"

Analisse approached me while Carla's mouth cooled. "Need somethin', babe?"

"It looked like you needed to get away from your old 'friend' there." I kept my voice to a whisper while I held up a T-shirt that said I'M THIS MANY TIMES FORTY. A large middle finger pointed up. Actually, I was forty-three.

Analisse tilted her head. "That obvious?"

I put the T-shirt back on the table and shrugged.

"Thanks, sweetie. Just call me if you really do need anything. I'll come running." I felt the radiant warmth of her palm as she patted the arm of my suit. She went on to another customer.

I found a black T-shirt with simple print. OVERWORKED AND UNDERFUCKED. I blurted a laugh then swiveled my head from side to side quickly as I reined in my response. I visualized Jess's tight face. The shirt would have shocked her anyway, but that I might wear it would probably make her pass out. Though she'd wanted me to loosen up, she'd have found this a bridge too far.

The message rang true, as it had been a year since the

breakup. It would have been true a year and a half before, but that's another story.

I was sure the other customers were staring at me, a poseur pervert in a crisp suit, eyeing up a nasty T-shirt. It took me a few minutes and a strained swallow or two until I finally worked up the nerve to take it to the register. I set it, print side down, on the counter.

Analisse nodded. "Find something?"

"Guess so."

She spread the T-shirt out and laughed. "I love this one." Her wide smile displayed large, bright teeth and a broad tongue that supported a post through the center of it. Despite the dark make-up, tattoos, piercings and deathly pale skin, she was strangely adorable. She delicately folded the T-shirt with its message facing up and winked. "I hope it isn't true."

"Well…" I can only imagine how uncool I looked while my mouth gaped, waiting for clever words to come. They didn't.

"Can I get you anything else?"

I looked into those intense eyes like a startled rabbit. Her eyes widened as she waited for an answer. Her tattooed hand hovered at the mouth of the bag with the neatly folded T-shirt. "Uh, no—I'm good." She set the T-shirt inside, took my money and counted out the change. Her warm hand lingered in my palm for a moment.

The bag hung with my bag of dress shirts like an uneven pair of testicles.

Goddamned if I'd ever wear that shirt. I even thought of throwing it away right on top of my Italian ice cup. I looked up to see Analisse talking to a coworker, and again our eyes met. She raised her brow like a drawbridge.

I shrugged.

Her full black lips curled into a grin.

I lingered in a couple of stores that catered to my sort, bought nothing, and finally departed the mall. The rattling crescendo of new construction focused as the doors opened. I took in the smell of stale tobacco, diesel fumes and sweet humidity on the summer air. I paused one more time by a trash can at the edge of the parking lot and separated the salacious T-shirt bag from my more appropriate ones. A back door to one of the stores opened. I turned to see purple hair, a black T-shirt, tribal tattoos, faded jeans, and a head that glimmered like a constellation. Her face pivoted slowly toward me as she lit up her cigarette. She gave a cute Hello Kitty curled finger wave as streams of smoke descended from her nostrils.

I laughed and waved back. My heart competed with the puffing jackhammer and buckling concrete. Her grin widened. "What the hell," I said to myself under my breath. I walked over to Analisse. "Can I bum one?" I nodded toward her Marlboro Light.

"You smoke?"

"Well, not much since college." Okay, truth was, not at all since college. Jess would never have had it.

Analisse flicked the box open and tapped one out. I took it in my hand and she held out a hot pink Bic lighter. I puffed, careful not to inhale, then I drew a bit in my lungs. I felt dizzy as I choked on the blue smoke. Analisse snatched the cigarette from between my fingers as I caught my breath. "Smoking doesn't agree with you."

I composed myself. "Guess it's been longer than I thought." I felt so stupid that I just started to turn away.

"I'm on a break." She drew another deep puff, then sent a stream of smoke out over her shoulder, away from me.

I stopped. I had to fight the words out. "Can I—can I buy you dinner?"

"Not hungry. Check that, not *very* hungry."

I puzzled as she widened her eyes for emphasis. Her nipples poked out like it was ten degrees, not ninety-five, and the message upon the T-shirt that I had bought crossed my mind. I looked out into the parking lot at my sensible gray Mercury. The words exploded out of my mouth before I could stop them. "You want to go for a drive?"

She planted both our cigarettes in the sand filled metal ash can. "Yup."

We crossed the lot, and she rested her arm on the hot roof as I hit the remote unlock button.

"Look I—don't do things like this," I said quietly.

She winked slyly. "Like what?"

"I—I mean—you know—like—well..."

Analisse laughed as she opened her door. "Me either, but you're such a fuckin' cutie. I just can't resist—taking a chance."

The oven heat of the interior warmed her musk perfume. She stretched her arms over her head and arched her back, exposing her trim stomach with its pierced belly button. A hint of savory sweat colored the air as I started the car.

I casually turned my hard-on to a comfortable position while she opened her window.

We drove along the back of the mall where a small access road led to the remains of an ill-fated strip mall. I parked in the back as if I had planned it. Quite the contrary. We stared at each other. Her eyes probed, probably to see if I was going to do anything. I stared at my hand, then eased it across the seats and rested it behind her neck. She licked her lips, opening them slightly.

I kissed her. It was a soft kiss for one second, maybe two. Her tongue was long and broad, with taste buds that felt like sandpaper. She pinned me back in the corner where the seat met the driver's side door.

She tasted of wintergreen Tic Tacs and fresh cigarettes. The backside of the post in her lip rattled along my lower teeth. The one in her tongue tickled as it traced the roof of my mouth, then sliced beneath my tongue.

I realized that my jacket and pants were open. Her right hand coiled around my rod as she thrust even deeper into my mouth. I'd never gotten, or given, a kiss like it. I was so hard it hurt.

Deliciously.

Her hand cradled my tight scrotum.

I slid my fingers up her shirt and squeezed one breast.

"Harder."

"Hmm?"

"Harder!"

I firmed my grip and she moaned her satisfaction. "Ooh." I gently pulled at the post through her left nipple. "Yeah!" She pushed me back in the seat and wiped her glossy lower lip with the side of her thumb. "Relax."

As stunned as I was, there was a part of me that could not relinquish control. "No, you relax." I pushed her back into the passenger seat and yanked her T-shirt up to her shoulders. She gave an approving moan as I nibbled at each nipple, tugging the posts while my hand sneaked into her tight jeans. Suddenly she seemed docile and obedient as she unbuttoned and unzipped her pants. Her body stiffened as I traced her pussy lips, softly flicking yet another post. She was soaking wet, and her hips began to rock while I massaged her pussy. Still, she gripped both my shoulders in her hands and tried to push me back to my seat. Her arms went slack as my fingers entered her.

After a bit of my exploring, her eyes and mouth went wide. I knew that look from the first time I'd found it on Jess.

The G-spot. G as in glorious.

Her hips rocked and her eyes went distant. The self-satisfaction of deep control poured over me. Jess had never responded like this.

Analisse was not done yet. She stroked my rod with a strange, twisting motion. The feeling was intoxicating. My control over her faded like a sunset. My hand went limp in her pants. She gently pressed me back to my seat and opened my tie and shirt. Her head eclipsed my cock as she descended over the console between the seats. She puddled my pants at my feet, spread my legs and eased her mouth over the tip.

"Oh, Jesus!"

Analisse struggled to navigate around the steering wheel. I pushed the button down at my side, and the seat hummed as it slid back as far as it could go. I released the lever at the side of the steering wheel and it swung up. "That's better." The posts in her tongue and lip teased all around my cock. At some point my left hand had been squeezed from her jeans and was now laced in her purple hair.

She lovingly licked every inch of my shaft with her rough tongue.

Jess's idea of fellatio had been to give just enough to get me down between her legs. There were long nights negotiating her terms of service.

"Oh, my—fuck!" I couldn't remember the last time I'd said fuck. But I repeated it several more times for good measure.

Analisse's mouth covered the tip as one hand squeezed my balls gently. Her other hand twisted up and down along with her wet mouth's luxurious travels down the top of my shaft. She increased the pressure as my balls tightened under each deliberate squeeze. I could feel my cock begin to twitch. The urgency of a powerful orgasm loomed.

In my earliest days with Jess, she had complained of my lack of restraint. I had only been good for a few minutes at best. I took her complaints to heart, and within a few months we could start at ten p.m. and not finish until two a.m. Even the demanding Jess had been impressed.

The sweat poured down my face, pooled along my collarbone and in my belly button. My toes and fingers clenched. My hard-fought restraint only seemed to challenge Analisse. She pushed me relentlessly as I focused everything I had on holding back. She stopped and looked deep in my eyes. She bit her lip and studied me. Determination spread over her face and she propped up on her knees, arched her back over the console, and gripped my balls like a lioness supporting her cub. She kissed along the bottom of my rod gently then pulled my tight balls upward. She sucked one testicle into her mouth. The post poking it made me gasp like I was diving in cold water on a hot day.

Her fingers squeezed like tiny, hungry boa constrictors around my cock while her mouth sucked each testicle alternately. A sharp ribbon of semen fired up my chest. I pulled a deep breath and fought against letting any more free. She took my cock into her mouth and squeezed my cool balls tightly. I writhed with a sudden whole-body orgasm. An echo of my detached voice returned from the back wall of the dead shopping center. She drew her mouth up and down as I drained in her. She flicked the last contractions from the tip with her tongue, then wiped her chin with a tea-and-crumpets swish of her fingertips.

I gripped the back of her neck and kissed her deeply, tasting me on her mouth. The combined flavors were delicious. Her body went limp as I shoved my tongue deep. I started to push my fingers back into her panties.

"Oh—I hate to say this, but I gotta get back to work."

I shook my head and dipped farther into her soaked pubic hair.

She gently pulled my hand out and laid it on her stomach. She patted my wet fingers. "Really, hon." She collapsed her palms to my face and kissed me then zipped her jeans.

"I—I feel bad that I didn't—that you—"

"I love the way you fought letting go. That was so fuckin' hot. I'll gladly take a rain check." She pulled a tube from her pocket and refreshed her black lipstick.

I shook my head defiantly. Her eyes traveled down my open shirt to my sated penis. Propriety rushed in, and I quickly buttoned my shirt then forced the tails into my pants. "Okay, it's a deal. I owe you."

She grinned and winked.

Jess spotted me jogging through the park. We often crossed paths there. But this time she stopped dead in her tracks as she read my black T-shirt. She turned and ran along with me. "I can't believe you're wearing that. It's—It's—"

"Isn't it great?"

"Uh, well—" She jogged faster to keep up with my increasing pace. Conflict ran over her face. I could have sworn I'd seen that expression during better days: surprise, desire, wanting me, briefly. But I realized just how hard she had been to read. I realized how little I wanted to read her now. I'd worked so hard to please her over the years, taken every responsibility, and never seemed to reach the destination. Too soft, not soft enough. Too fast, not fast enough.

For the first time, I was glad that Jess had left me. Now I sped up more and left her far behind. She never could keep up with me, but I'd never really run away.

As I walked it off at my apartment, I swiped the sweat from my brow and gulped a Powerade. I looked down at my nasty black T-shirt. It really was the only thing that went with the three pairs of comfortable black sweatpants I'd recently bought. I needed more to go with them.

It was Tuesday evening. I picked up my keys and set out for the mall.

FELLATIO: A LOVE STORY

Scarlett French

He never asked me to go down on him, not once, even though I know he loved it. He knew how I felt, knew I couldn't, knew that the messages I'd picked up from porn were that men thought, *Yeah, suck it bitch.* I think I'd even heard those very words used—and that was in some stupid mainstream film. It wasn't that I'd had a bad experience, it was simply about the messages I'd picked up from popular culture. We had talked about it. He told me that if a man is disrespectful in his thoughts toward his partner during a blow job, then he's disrespectful in his thoughts during the missionary position. He told me it's about the man, not the act. It was a logical argument and I agreed with him in principle, but it didn't change how I felt. So he never asked, never hinted, and he never scrimped on going down on me.

And it was because he never asked, never hinted, and never scrimped, that two years later I found myself in a bookshop one Friday night, holding Violet Blue's *Ultimate Guide to Fellatio,* skimming its contents. You've got to understand two things about me: one, I try to be a fair person, and two, I'm contrary. So, because he kept giving to me all that time, and because he never once tried to make me do what I didn't want to do, I found myself wanting to confront my negativity about blow jobs. And because these things proved his respect and love for me, I found myself buying that book.

I rushed home; we were living together by this stage.

"Honey," I said, "I've bought a book on fellatio."

"Oh?" he replied, his tone ambiguous, perhaps aiming for neutrality.

"I'm just going to see what it says, that's all."

"Look, you don't have to do it," he said, "you make up for it in other ways, you give to me in other ways."

"Well, I'm just going to see what it says." I kissed him. "Night-night. I'm going to bed to read."

I opened the book to chapter one, braced for advice that if you want to keep your man you'd better blow him. What I found instead was an introduction to the psychology of fellatio. My hackles immediately softened as I realized this writer wasn't going to tell me what my obligations were. Instead, she described the joys of cocksucking: how connecting it can be, how horny, and what a gift it is. She wrote that if you've been disrespected by a lover on this count, you've been disrespected by that lover in most things—evaluate whether that's the kind of relationship you want to have. Just like what he'd said. That most men don't approach any kind of sex with a desire to disrespect, but rather to connect, or at least have fun. And for those few who do, well, it's an indictment of them, not any sex act. I continued on through chapter two, about anatomy, and on past safe sex, hygiene, and genital massage, and then I arrived at oral techniques. The text was peppered throughout with erotica about fellatio and to my surprise, I found myself getting wet. Very wet, in fact. By the time I reached the deep-throating section—chapter nine—my hand had slid down my belly and was stroking my clit as I educated myself about the techniques. I imagined opening my throat and pacing my breathing to take him all in. I thought of calling him into the bedroom, or going out to join him on the sofa, but I came suddenly and powerfully under my own hand and decided that I wanted to sleep on it, take some time to assimilate this new information. Curled up asleep some time later, I felt him slip into bed beside me, his body warm against my back. His arm encircled me, and I shifted my body to snuggle in against him.

In the morning, I woke to the sound of his breathing, deep and rhythmic. His arm was still around me, and I felt the twitch of his morning erection against my arse. I smiled lazily and thought about backing up against it as I so often did, about becoming wet instantly for him, and sliding my pussy against his cock until he woke enough to slip his delicious length between my thighs while we both continued to lie side by side, slowly thrusting ourselves to a fully awake state and coming together, an appetite awakener for some vigorous weekend sex later in the day. But as the previous night's reading sprang to mind, I hesitated. Instead, I imagined my mouth on his cock, and I felt a spasm in my cunt. *Yes,* I decided. *Yes, I want to do this.* I pulled the covers back gently and surveyed his solid brown body, the broad chest and rounded pecs, the softness of his belly, the treasure trail to his pubic hair, his cock hard against his slumbering thighs. I pushed him onto his back, and he sighed through his sleepiness as I began to kiss his chest, working my way down his body.

As I rasped my tongue over his thighs, his eyes flashed open in surprise. I smiled at his beautiful sleep-softened face. "I've been doing some reading," was all I said, and I went back to licking my way across his thighs. His legs parted a little. I looked up to find his eyes still fixed on me. In the book, I'd read how horny it can be for a man to see his lover relishing his cock, staring playfully back at him while she uses her mouth to play with his dick. I curled my hand around his cock and steadied it with my fist. It pulsated lightly in my hand. A tiny droplet of precome appeared at its tip and to my surprise, I wasn't put off. With my finger, I circled the head, spreading the lube across its surface. He moaned as I stroked the seam on the underside of the head. "Oh, you like that baby?" I cooed. "Well, how about I use my tongue?"

His eyes widened as my face approached his hard member. I brought my tongue out slowly and licked my lips deliberately before making that first contact with his shaft. The skin was soft on my tongue. I liked the way it felt. I licked all the way up from the base to the tip. It didn't taste bad at all, not even the precome, and I'd always been squeamish about tasting come. I kept my tongue out, curved it, and pushed it down the shaft again, then back up. He made a strange sound that was somewhere between a whimper and a growl. His eyes rolled back a bit, and I felt a surge of excitement ripple through me. I encircled the head with swirling licks until I felt myself wanting to take his whole cock in my mouth—much like when I wanted him in my cunt so bad I'd physically ache. To my surprise, it was with that same urgency, that same desire. I licked the whole shaft, covering it with my saliva. Then I smiled at him, licked my lips, and kept my eyes on his as best I could as I sunk my mouth down over his whole cock, devouring it from tip to base. As I took him all the way into my mouth, I felt my pussy surge with wetness, my muscles clenching involuntarily. I breathed through the gag reflex when I felt the tip of his cock in the back of my throat and pushed a little farther still, to get all of him inside my mouth. He moaned from in his gut, and his face took on a beatific expression. "Mmm," I mumbled, my mouth absolutely full of his cock. I knew the sound would cause subtle vibrations against him, but I also wanted him to know that I liked what I was doing.

I sucked lightly as I pulled back up, releasing him, then slid back down, taking care to toy with the head on my way. His whole body was flexing and my cunt was clenching and tingling simultaneously. But as much as I would have liked nothing more than to straddle him now and slide my hot, open cunt down on his hard, slick cock and ride it, I also wanted to finish what I'd started; this revelation, this...joy. The delicious torture of my empty cunt spurred me on to keep sucking, keep filling my mouth completely with his dick until I was slamming my mouth repeatedly against his mound, his pubic hair tickling my nose with each stroke. I breathed as I'd read about in the book and each time took it deep into the back of my throat so there wasn't a millimeter of his cock that wasn't contained by my mouth, the warm walls sliding against it, sucking it, at first gently and then harder and harder as I found myself wanting to milk him, wanting him to come.

"Oh, god, oh, god, honey. Oh, I'm going to come soon, I..." I kept up the rhythm without abating, knowing I could handle what was about to happen. I felt a rippling along the underside of his cock and knew that his orgasm was on its way. I felt his body tense and raise up at the waist. "Ahhhnnh," he cried, as I felt his warm come shoot out and fill my mouth. He fell back down on the bed, twitching all over. I managed to swallow a little before the gag reflex kicked in, despite my best efforts. I coughed hard and made a choking sound, a bit like a cat being sick. A small puddle of his come was now pooled between his hip and pubic hair. I looked up, horrified. His dreamy expression turned into a grin until we were both shaking with laughter.

"Sorry about that!" I said finally, serious now. It isn't exactly flattering to have someone cough up your love juice like it's poison.

"Come here," he said, "and don't worry about it at all."

I came up alongside him and flopped my head down on the pillow, facing him. He stared at me for a long time, smiling. "It was wonderful. Thank you," he said softly, his eyes bright with love. It may sound strange that he thanked me, but we have this thing about courtesy—that a relationship shouldn't be exempt from politeness. If anything, your partner is the person you should want to be most polite to.

I kissed him. "Well, it really was my pleasure," I replied. He kissed me back fully, slipping his tongue in.

"I can taste myself in your mouth," he whispered. His hand slipped between my thighs, and I spread my legs for him. "You're so wet!" he exclaimed.

"Well, I guess it turns out I like fellatio," I said with a grin.

He stroked my clit, then slipped two fingers into my pussy. I sighed deeply, my cunt muscles pulsing around his fingers. As he moved them inside me, my body bucked slightly.

"God, you really could just come, couldn't you?"

"Mmmhmm," I answered.

"What would you like, honey?" he asked.

"Fuck me," I answered.

"You asked for it," he said.

Now it was my turn to be pushed onto my back. He climbed on top of me and brought his face close to mine, kissing my lips as he pushed his still-hard cock into my slippery cunt. I engulfed him hungrily, just like I had moments ago with my mouth. "Ohhhh," I sighed. His cock felt so fucking good inside me, so delicious. I put my hands on his ass, getting off on the motion of his body as he drove his dick into me. "Just fuck me, baby, just give it to me," I cried. He began to thrust into me hard, every stroke deep and focused. I raised my hips up and thrust back in perfect rhythm, increasing the intensity. I was so wet for him, so on fire, waves of pleasure rushed through me. Only seconds later I came hard, his beautiful cock buried deep inside me, my hips bucking against him, the smell of our sex in my nostrils.

We lay together in dreamy silence for a long time. Finally he turned to me, shaking his head slowly. "When you set your mind on something, you do it with gusto, don't you?"

"Let's just say I had a change of heart. That book showed me that we were both missing out."

"Well, I can't pretend I'm not delighted," he grinned. "You gave me such pleasure, I can't even describe it."

"You'll get plenty of chances to find the right words," I said, as I began to kiss his chest again, working my way down. "After all, practice makes perfect."

LOGIC

Jacqueline Applebee

ogic tells me that I should not be here. The loud voice that rings out, however, is not logical.

"Yes! Ah, yes."

Sammie pinches Paul's nipples right through his shirt, as we stand on the doorstep to his home. His accented cries remind me of an awful porn film that Sammie and I watched once, a long time ago. She dared me to sit through it all, and I did it, just to see her smile. When she asked me to come with her tonight, I tried to refuse, but I am ultimately powerless with her.

I've known Sammie for years. She is my best friend, and we're as close as sisters. We've never been lovers, but we care for each other deeply. When she asked me to go with her to Paul's apartment, it wasn't logic that made me agree. It was something far stronger.

You see, Sammie never blows her boyfriends. I've known this fact for almost as long as I've known her—that she usually finds blow jobs distasteful. She must have overcome her issues though;

what to do with her teeth, should she spit or swallow? Something major must have changed for the better, for her to be even contemplating going down on her guy. I admired her wanting to try this, but wished she could do it a thousand miles away. I didn't want to bear witness to the strength of her feelings for Paul, because I feared it would cost me the feelings I had for her.

I step over the threshold and into Paul's home. The place is beautiful; of course, it has to be. As I walk through the living room, I smell coconut and faint spices. Piles of colorful North African cookbooks sit on a table, and I wonder idly if Paul tastes like lamb tagine? He has lots of space in his home, with tasteful furnishings, and the loveliest light fixture I have ever seen, hanging in the middle of his bedroom. I stand beneath the very masculine chandelier and admire the curls of steel. Each strand of hard metal twists this way and that, like the possibilities that course through my ever-so-logical brain. Every way I look at it, my being here is a mistake.

Paul and Sammie lie back on the bed, and I join them. I feel stiff and awkward. Three into two doesn't go—everyone knows that. So what am I still doing here?

I can't help but look at Paul as he flushes when Sammie kisses him. He looks so young, so innocent, and he is everything I am not. He is tall, slim, and exotically continental. His words are tinged with the most beautiful Dutch accent. He has fair brown hair, soft blue eyes, and a loud belly laugh. He also has a powerful voice when he is enjoying himself, even if all he seems to say is "Yes."

I, on the other hand, am round, brown, and female. Sammie is not into women, and there is nothing about me that she could want in this special way. My jealousy is making me sick. I don't want to let her go, even though I know that I have no claim. Paul makes Sammie happy, and no matter how I try, I cannot deny it. Now she wants to make the Dutchman of her dreams happy too, so who am I to stand in her way?

"Come on, I can't do this without you," she whines and wheedles until I finally give in.

Logic tells me to just leave Sammie and Paul to it, that they don't need me here.

"Show me how to blow Paul," Sammie whispers as her silent boyfriend unzips his pants. "You love giving blow jobs. Show me how to be as good as you."

This is not an insult. It's true that I pride myself on my cock-sucking skills. I've enjoyed the look on men's faces when I've blown them—loved the way they try to hang on, to make it last and draw out every drop of pleasure. I've seen their heads thrown back almost in agony, felt them thrust into me with aggressive passion, and then sag boneless, unable to even speak when they finally come. I've reveled in my expertise at being a premier cock-lover, but I never wanted to suck dick the way I wanted to devour my friend. Logic tells me that Sammie would be appalled at my feelings for her.

"It's not something I can easily do, Sammie." I will myself not to stand up and walk right out.

"But it's possible, isn't it?" The hopeful tinge in her voice makes me melt; I am weak for this woman. My mind searches for some way to make this happen, and I quickly formulate a plan. I have to do a good job; she trusts me an awful lot right now, and I cannot let her down.

"Give me your hand."

Sammie places her beautiful brown fingers in mine, and I kiss her wrist. She smells of cocoa butter, her touch is so soft, and I never want to stop feeling it.

"Whatever I do to your hand, do it to Paul's cock," I instruct her quietly. Sammie hesitates for a moment, and then flicks a look at me. Big brown eyes reflect my worried face, and I feel ashamed. I am doing this for her. Everything is for her.

Paul looks up at me, too. A touch of apprehension skitters over his features. Sammie loves this man, and I love Sammie. Logic dictates that I should love Paul, too, if only by proxy.

I kiss her wrist once more, and she leans down to kiss the base of her lover's cock. We both listen as he takes a breath, tenses, and then sighs out loud. I lick around Sammie's pulse point with long wet circles. Her small pink tongue laps around the column of Paul's flesh.

"Ya," he sighs, and his soft Dutch accent makes me tingle with unexpected longing. My teeth gently run over the ball of Sammie's hand, over the soft swell of flesh beneath her thumb. I glide my face against her hand and read her palm with my lips. Sammie is going to have a long and happy life. She has so much love ahead of her. I blink back tears. I can't hate either of them for this.

The salt I taste a moment later does not come from my eyes; Sammie perspires as she works Paul's cock deeper into her mouth.

Logic may tell me that there's no such thing as destiny, but as I lick her hand like a supplicant, I don't much care about logic. The feel of her finger is more intense than any mathematical theory. Logic can kiss my big black ass.

I suck her middle finger into my mouth, slurping as if she were chocolate ice cream. The phrase *Dutch cocoa* pops into my head and I sigh.

Sammie's a quick study; I almost sense her mouth relaxing as she pushes her lips over the bulbous head of Paul's cock. She sucks her new man like he's the last glass of ice water before we all go to hell. She bolts him down—too fast, too much, way too soon. Her head bobs away at full speed, and she becomes a blur before me.

I press my teeth into Sammie's flesh, and she whips her head up sharply. The flash of anger I see for a moment tells me how annoyed she is at the interruption.

"He'll last five seconds if you keep that up. Do you want a quickie, or do you want him to scream when he explodes in you?" I chastise her. I incline my head and give her a look that says to listen to the expert.

Sammie looks from Paul to me. Her fingers return to my face, and I breathe out a relieved sigh. I sweep my tongue over her fingertips, pulling slightly as I go. She does the same with Paul's cock, and he gasps and pants noisily.

"Make him wetter," I urge roughly, and soon his cock is shiny, glistening with her spit. He reflects the glow of the ornate light fixture. The spirals of hard metal mirror all three of us on ever-twisting surfaces. We all look up and see each other for what feels like the first time.

Sammie's fingers enter me again. I suck hard as I swallow her length into my wet mouth. She groans, Paul groans, and I buck against her. I meet Paul's hungry gaze at that moment, and logic tells me what he needs. Logic tells me that Paul and I are essentially the same, that we are both afraid of losing Sammie. Her friend and her lover should not be competing. We both love her so much.

I slide down lower onto the big bed, still with Sammie's fingers in my mouth. She adjusts herself, so she doesn't lose contact with me. The fingers of my free hand press against Paul's lips, and he sucks me inside without hesitation. His tongue curls around my fingers. Paul sucks me, I suck Sammie, and Sammie sucks Paul. This is the pattern the future will take. We haven't lost anything; each of us has gained at least one other lover, and I have gained two.

Paul's eyes roll back in his head, Sammie's fingers pop out of my mouth, and in a heartbeat she shoves them under the band of my knickers. Her fingers press into my pussy—I am soaking wet, and she slips inside with ease. She glides into me, as Paul's cock slides into her pussy, and the rhythm is unbroken by the change in action. I hump Sammie's hand, grind against her until I see stars in the chandelier above me.

Now that my mouth is free, I make sounds that are illogical and crazy. I feel my orgasm building, and I give in to the burning quake that rolls through me, until I come hard, sobbing out both of their names. My fingers yank out of Paul's mouth as I explode. I don't know where I am.

The instant Sammie pulls out of me, Paul grabs her sticky hand, and I watch with amazement as he presses it to his face and then puts it into his mouth. He sucks my moisture from her fingers, smearing his face, licking her hand clean, and then he comes with a glass-shattering scream, pulsing and spraying us both with his spunk. Logic tells me I am in heaven.

Sammie's lips are upon me, and she kisses me with such ferocity that I almost weep. She holds me as the aftershocks ripple through my body, and suddenly Paul rises up above us. His long arms encircle us both, and he murmurs in that beautiful, infuriating language of his. He pulls Sammie backward until they both lie down. Logic is spent. Instinct takes over. I descend on my new lovers. Paul spreads Sammie's legs wider and uses his long fingers to present her for me. I suck her pussy and lick her juices that mix with the dribbles of Paul's come. I taste North Africa in their fusion—sweet apricots, buttery couscous, and potent spices. I devour both of them, and I don't know where one ends and the other begins. We writhe and swirl together like the chandelier that hangs above us, but there are no hard edges tonight. We are united in sticky sweetness. Sammie comes at last, clenching her dripping thighs around my head, and a new world is born from her hoarse cries. We are a mess of tangled limbs, hot and flushed, but we all grin at each other, at the new magical thing we have just done.

Logic says that I should never have come here tonight. But as we all curl against each other, falling into a deep and happy sleep, I know that logically, there was no other place I could be.

FROSTED

Kristina Wright

have cinnamon rolls."

No response.

"Big fluffy cinnamon rolls with luscious cream cheese frosting," I singsonged. "Your favorite."

There was a slight rustling under the sheets and a barely audible, "Huh?" to let me know Sam, my flu-recovering boyfriend, was still alive.

"C'mon, Sam," I said. "I went out in this snowstorm to bring you cinnamon rolls."

Sam pulled the covers from his head and gave me a sleepy grin. "Did you go out like that?"

I looked down at my flannel pajamas, the ones with bright green frogs dancing across the hot-pink fabric. "Well, I put on a coat. It's like ten freakin' degrees out there. I deserve a little appreciation."

He propped himself up on the pillows and looked at me expectantly. "Thanks, babe."

I plopped the box of gooey cinnamon rolls on his stomach and climbed under the covers beside him. "You're welcome. Now you have to warm me up."

"Damn, you're freezing!"

I ignored him and snuggled up against his naked body. He grumbled a little, but he tucked me against his shoulder with one arm while negotiating the bakery box with the other. "Oh, my, god, these smell incredible."

He was practically moaning, and I was just a little bit jealous. Okay, maybe more than a little bit.

"You've been sick for two weeks, of course they smell good," I said. "I figured you deserved a treat."

He kissed my forehead absentmindedly, and I might as well have been invisible. Sam loves cinnamon rolls. Not just any cinnamon rolls, mind you, but those enormous bakery cinnamon rolls filled with gobs of sticky cinnamon sugar and covered with an inch of cream cheese frosting. I've seen Sam devour two of the things in twenty minutes flat. A box of six wouldn't last a week.

Sam was halfway through his first cinnamon roll and pawing through the box. "No extra frosting?"

"You don't need it," I said. "Those things are practically dripping in frosting."

He made a face. "I *like* the frosting. It's the best part."

I dragged my finger across the top of the cinnamon roll he was holding and slowly licked the glob of frosting from my finger. "You know, I read somewhere that cinnamon is an aphrodisiac."

Sam ignored me, eyes closed and head against the pillows, as he savored the rest of his cinnamon roll.

I was getting annoyed now. Eating wasn't the only thing Sam hadn't been doing much of for the past couple of weeks. I waited until he'd devoured the last bite and then elbowed him in the ribs. "Hey, you."

He looked at me, his eyelids heavy with lust, but not lust for me. Lust for baked goods. Lust for cinnamon and cream cheese frosting. "Hmm?"

"I said, I heard cinnamon is an aphrodisiac."

"Yeah?" He was listening, but only barely. The five remaining cinnamon rolls were calling to him like caloric sirens, and I was only seconds away from losing his attention again. "You did?"

"Yeah, I did." I leaned over the side of the bed, digging through my coat, which I had dropped on the floor. I retrieved what I was looking for and tucked it under the covers. "What do you think?"

Sam looked at me, eyes narrowed. "I think you're up to something."

"Who me?" I asked, all wide-eyed innocence, as sweet as the cinnamon rolls Sam coveted. "I was just trying to get my boyfriend's attention."

"Yeah, right. What do you have under there, Kelly?"

"Nothing," I said, ducking farther down under the covers and knowing he'd come after me.

I was right, he did. I shrieked with laughter as he tickled me, but I hung on to my prize.

"Give it up," he growled, nibbling my neck in a way that would make me utterly helpless to resist him. "I'm going to win."

He smelled like cinnamon and cream cheese frosting and pure manly goodness. I gasped for breath, pushing at him with my shoulder until he backed off. "Okay, okay! I give up."

"So what is it?"

I pulled my hand from under the covers and showed him the plastic container.

"Extra frosting!" He tickled me again. "You've been holding out on me."

"Stop! Stop!" I tucked my head down and curled up into a ball until he quit. "This isn't for your cinnamon rolls," I said.

"What's it for then?"

I reached under the covers with my free hand and gave his growing erection a squeeze. All our wrestling around had gotten him turned on. He wasn't the only one. I had been hot and bothered for at least a week.

"I was thinking that maybe cinnamon rolls aren't the only things that taste good covered in cream cheese frosting."

He grinned. "You are bad."

"No, I'm good. Very, very good." I pushed the sheet and comforter down, exposing his thick, beautiful cock in all its rigid glory.

"I know," he murmured, not even acknowledging the fact that his precious box of cinnamon rolls had landed on the carpet with a thud. "I vaguely remember."

"I guess I should remind you what you've been missing while you've been convalescing, hmm?"

I stroked his cock ever so lightly, feeling it jump against my hand. It had been two long, lonely weeks, and I was going to enjoy Sam's recovery very, very much. I popped the lid off the container and licked the frosting with the tip of my tongue.

Sam groaned. "Do that to me."

"In a minute." The frosting was thick, sweet, and creamy, almost cloying. I turned the little container upside down and rubbed it over the head of Sam's cock. He jumped.

"That's cold," he complained, but he didn't push me away.

I pushed the container of frosting down farther, until it looked as if his cock was wearing a funny-looking hat. Neither of us was laughing, though. Slowly, I pulled the container away, leaving the head of his cock covered in frosting that was beginning to melt from his body heat.

"Oh, my, that looks good," I whispered. My mouth was watering, and it wasn't for the frosting.

"Please, babe," Sam pleaded softly. His cock twitched, waiting for me, for my mouth.

I lowered my head over him, my hair brushing his stomach and thighs. I took him between my lips without touching him with my hands. We both groaned, though mine was muffled. I lapped at his cock, tasting the slick sweetness of his precome even through the thick, creamy frosting. The two tastes and textures were heaven on my tongue.

Sam tangled his hands in my hair, guiding me slowly on his cock. I was happy he wasn't in a hurry because I intended to take my time going down on him. A very long time.

I popped the head of his cock out my mouth and stroked the length of his shaft. "Yummy."

"Oh, yeah," he breathed.

I dipped two fingers into the frosting container and smeared his shaft with the sticky sweetness. Then I fisted his cock, jerking him off as I licked the frosting that accumulated on the swollen tip as I stroked him.

The more aroused Sam gets, the quieter he gets. The only sounds in the room were me sucking, slurping, and stroking his cock, so I knew I had his full, undivided, very aroused attention. Over and over, I licked him, pausing only to apply more frosting. It wasn't the best lubricant, but Sam was leaking precome like crazy and I was getting him pretty juicy with my saliva, so his cock was a sticky, wet, delicious mess.

"You're driving me crazy," he gasped, as I took him as far into my mouth as I could.

I pulled back, mumbling around the head of his cock, "Good."

Without freeing himself from my mouth, Sam reached down and put his hand between my legs. "You've soaked through your pants." His cock twitched in my mouth as if it had a life of its own. "Damn, baby. You're so wet."

I wiggled against his hand, urging him to touch me. I had no intention of stopping what I was doing, but I didn't mind a little reward for my efforts. Sam pushed his hand down the front of my pajama pants and into my panties. His fingers stroked my swollen clit and I gasped around his cock. I pushed against his hand, sucking him to the same rhythm with which he stroked me.

"So wet," he said. "I wonder what your pussy would taste like covered in frosting?"

I whimpered, imagining his mouth on me, my wet, swollen pussy covered in cream cheese frosting. My hard little clit like a ripe cherry on top of all that sweetness. I popped the head of his cock from my mouth long enough to say, "Later. I want to taste you."

I slid him back into my mouth, swirling my tongue around the head of his cock and capturing the last creamy taste of frosting. Then he pushed two fingers into my wetness and rubbed my G-spot. I gasped, losing my rhythm in the process. Impatiently, I pushed his hand away.

"Stop distracting me," I said, licking the sugary head of his cock once more. "I'll get mine later. I want you to come in my mouth."

Sam moaned, which was enough to let me know he was fine with waiting to satisfy me. He swelled and twitched between my lips, so close to orgasm his thighs were trembling. I held the head of his cock under my tongue as I stroked him into my mouth with both hands.

Gripping my hair tightly, Sam arched his hips off the bed

and pushed himself farther into my mouth. Then, with a soft moan and a pulse of his cock, he was coming. He tasted sweet, so sweet, and it had nothing to do with the frosting. I held him in place, sucking and swallowing as he throbbed in my mouth, until his body went limp. His cock stayed firm and I sucked him gently, reluctant to let him go. I giggled at his soft moans as he alternately clenched my hair tighter and tried to nudge me away from his overly sensitive cock.

"Stop," he gasped finally. "I can't take any more."

I slid up beside him, licking my lips. Truth be told, I felt a little sick from all the frosting I'd eaten, but it was well worth the relaxed and satisfied expression on Sam's face. "I'm not sure I'll ever look at cinnamon rolls the same way again."

Sam laughed. "It's worse for me. I'll never be able to go in the bakery again without getting a hard-on."

I held up the half-empty container of frosting. "Tell you what. I'll keep delivering the cinnamon rolls if you'll promise to make it worth my while."

His grin was nothing short of wicked. "Deal."

It was two hours before we got out of bed, and Cinnamon Roll Sunday became a weekly event.

LONG RELIEF

T. Hitman

In the dream, she was sucking his cock again, like she'd done a month ago in another town, another state. Only *sucking* wasn't exactly the right term for what she was doing; no, Emily was *making love* to it, to all eight rock-hard inches of Colin Pronger's manhood. She'd made every vein, bump—hell, every *hair* lining its shaft come alive. She was so good at pleasuring him with her tight, wet lips that the rest of Colin's six-foot-two frame of ropey, twenty-four-year-old muscles sang in appreciation. Gooseflesh broke over his arms. Electric pinpricks tingled across the soles of his size-twelve feet and between his bare toes. His balls, heavy with too much unejaculated batter, had melted into puddles of loose, sweaty flesh. Colin's body was on fire; his cock generated the heat. Its blood vessels had transformed into conduits pumping megawatts of electricity. Surely, he thought, something that felt this incredible couldn't be good for a man in regular doses, any more than it could be real.

That was the kicker. The *real* part. The last time Em had

hummed on his stick, he'd winced several times due to the scrape of her back teeth. She'd been unable to handle more than the fireman's helmet of his dick-head and a few inches of shaft, certainly not providing the balls-deep beauty he was presently enjoying. She hadn't gently handled his nuts—Colin's pride and joy, a set of low-hangers he'd shaved because she thought they smelled nasty up close, especially after a baseball game, and she didn't like to touch, let alone suck, them.

Over the course of the past month, Colin's nuts had itched something terrible, worse than the torture that nine innings locked in a jockstrap and cup normally unleashed upon a man's balls. The hair had grown back. The mouth wrapped around his cock had swallowed him all the way down to those itchy fuckers. And the owner of that mouth was happily playing with his sac without bitching about its ripeness.

No, Em was seven states and more than a thousand miles away, and she certainly had never given him this kind of quality blow job before. It was only an illusion, Colin told himself. He'd already humped his first wet dream in six years into the motel room's too-hard mattress after the team's arrival in Buffalo. It had woken him up, and only the sweaty mass of the pillow had prevented his howls from also waking Leyritz in the bed on the other side of the room. Playing baseball—any sport, for that matter—had a way of boosting a man's testosterone levels; Colin had walked around half-hard part of the time, fully erect the rest. A fuckin' wet dream, squirted into the sheets. And here he was again, dreaming of his girlfriend's mouth firmly clamped around his stick, moving up and down on him, and her hand fondling his nuts.

But Colin realized he wasn't wet-dreaming this sensation. He clearly felt the mattress beneath his shoulders, butt, and ankles. He was on his back, not his stomach, and though it was a possibility, humping air had never felt this incredibly realistic. A bead of sweat trickled out of Colin's buzz cut and down the side of his face. Its nagging itch anchored him back to reality: a double bed in a motel room with two such beds, and a sleeping teammate—fellow relief pitcher Joel Leyritz—crashed out a yard away.

Somebody *was* sucking Colin's dick!

He fought the urge to swipe at the hot, teasing trickle of perspiration, as well as to give in to the shudder that wanted to travel outward from his cock through his body in concentric circles of overwhelming pleasure, like the surface of a pond overcome by ripples. Colin needed to know more about the identity of the skilled set of lips worshipping his manhood, but he also couldn't risk having it end. Not this blow job. He'd never had one so fucking good.

A wet sucking cadence reached his ears over his heart's drumbeats. *Spit,* Colin thought. And judging by the way he normally flowed, a goodly amount of precome as well. The blast he'd fired into the mattress had soaked the bed beneath him, as though he'd pissed it instead of splattering it full of his seed.

The hand gently groping at his balls unexpectedly tugged harder. Somehow, Colin managed not to leap off his bed as fresh pleasure exploded through his insides. But his left leg jerked in response, and the mouth on his cock ceased sucking. He felt it slide off him, shocked away by his jolt of movement. The swampy breeze billowing out of the struggling air conditioner gusted over his dick-head and quickly dried his mysterious cocksucker's saliva. A hand carefully guided his member backward until it was resting across Colin's six-pack, its head reaching as far as the fur-ringed bullet hole of his belly button. To have dropped it outright would have reawakened the sleeper, someone seemed to have judged. His tool was so hard, so fucking heavy, letting it fall like that would have slapped an unconscious man out of a coma.

The fingers on his balls also withdrew their touch. Colin held his breath and realized the uninvited stranger was retreating. His cock ached. In silence, he cursed himself for breaking the rhythm, for scaring off his talented benefactor. Colin needed to come, and something told him that mysterious mouth wasn't going to deny him what all men seek when getting great head: it planned to swallow down his baby-makers. All he needed to do was to get it back to work.

It struck Colin exactly what had to be done to accomplish that goal. He let out a round of fake snores, and the ploy worked.

Slowly, tentatively feeling its way along the inside of his thigh, the stranger's fingers groped Colin's balls. For the few tense minutes his dick and the mouth were apart, Colin's steely member had lain swollen and bloated across his abdomen, gorged with blood and dripping precome into his navel. Another hand carefully lifted his thickness out of the sticky puddle. Colin tensed in anticipation. The warm brush of the stranger's tongue across his stomach threatened to launch him off the bed, but Colin stopped himself from moving completely. He wanted this mouth back on him as much as the mouth craved being there. And it obviously *did* want to, judging by the lusty licks over his precome soaked six-pack and pubes. It even went lower to swab the stink off his nuts—Colin guessed that between milking his dick, the stranger had savored the sweaty funk of his once-again-hairy balls.

Those theatrical snores filled Colin's nose with the acrid, masculine aroma bottled up in the motel room. Earlier in the day, not long after the team had exited the bus, he'd been paired up with Joel Leyritz. As the motel room's pungent air filled his lungs, intoxicating him—and the mouth on his erection sucked him closer to unloading—Colin replayed the afternoon's events.

Leyritz was twenty-seven, had been called up to the major league team twice in the past few seasons, but was basically playing for chump change compared to the going rate for pros making minimum wage in the big club. The guy loved the game; he'd been married for a couple of years and, after they'd checked into the motel, Colin had asked him about it.

"What's your wife think about you being on the road so much?"

"She don't mind it as much as me," Leyritz had chuckled in his husky voice. And then he'd squeezed down on the meaty lump between his legs, saying more with that one action than a whole mouthful of words.

Dinner had consisted of pizza and beer. After that, it was back to the motel for lights out in readiness for the next day's game. Unlike the big leaguers who got their own hotel suites, their own high-priced whores, and whatever else they wanted, Triple-A baseball grunts were lucky to get bargain motel rooms, pizza, and the pleasure of bunking with a teammate.

The air-conditioning sucked almost as strongly as the mouth on Colin's dick; he and Leyritz had quickly stunk up the place with a musty haze of sweating balls and bare feet.

Leyritz...

It struck Colin that the mysterious cock-gobbler clamped to his rod might be a lay that Leyritz kept on the ready in Buffalo. She'd sucked off his roommate and had then moved over to him. It didn't hit home that it could actually be Leyritz himself until Colin forced his eyelids up and peered through the slits.

It couldn't be! Joel Leyritz, kneeling at the side of his bed...

But it was.

The wan glow of the streetlight outside and the alarm clock's

LED revealed enough of his fellow relief pitcher's buzz cut for Colin to identify the expert set of lips presently slurping on his cock like their owner's life depended upon it. Colin even made out the perfect O of Leyritz's goatee and mustache, whose clippings littered the bathroom sink. Leyritz had trimmed his mug earlier that night but hadn't shaved his neck or cheeks; visiting players didn't shave before a game for the intimidation factor, even in the minors.

Colin's disbelieving eyes widened. He'd passed out in a pair of boxers; Leyritz had fished his dick and nuts out of the slit. The fucker had crossed a line with Colin no man before had ever dared. Colin liked pussy. *Loved* it. He didn't jones on other dudes.

Still...

Whatever rage he felt at having his balls licked and his tool swallowed whole by his married teammate quickly burned away. Colin had never experienced a blow job this magnificent, and he wasn't about to cut it short, any more than he had the power to prolong it. The room, already hot and sour to the point of discomfort, suddenly grew airless. All the power in Colin's body—along with what felt like the power of an exploding star—rushed through his cock, tickling his balls and teasing his toes, his nipples, and his asshole along the way. He stifled a grunt—calling out now could possibly drive Leyritz's mouth away from his dick right as it started to squirt, and he didn't want that.

If anything, that first spurt of juice made Leyritz suck harder, faster.

In a normal, perfect world, Colin would have grabbed the buzzed-clean back of his teammate's head, driven his dick all the way deep into his throat, and shouted a blue streak of insults.

Fuckin' cocksucker! Suck it to my hairy bull-balls, dude—and don't you dare miss a drop of my batter!

But he didn't, and even so, the amazing sensations that pinned his physical body to the bed while releasing his soul to levitate above the lumpy mattress were enough of a reward for playing it cool. Unable to resist, Colin smiled, exhaling a deep, appeased sigh as his climax crescendoed. After that brief instant of heaven, his joy powered down.

With his steel-hard, spent cock still in Leyritz's mouth, his eyes wide open and fresh sweat stinging at them, some unaffected part of Colin's dazed senses registered the wet gulping sound from between his legs. Leyritz swallowed his seed and hungrily licked at his gummed-up piss-hole before releasing Colin's deflating member, leaving it and his nuts hanging out of his fly.

Colin remained frozen on his back, his muscles aching. The wet stroking sound of Leyritz's hand on his own stick slithered up from the side of the bed. It didn't take long; after a few tense seconds, Colin heard a muffled grunt. In his mind's eye, he imagined Leyritz nutting his yogurt across the worn carpeting. The idea made his cock swell again and his balls itch. He needed more relief, and desperately so.

But Leyritz snuck back to his side of the room, and while Colin's dick throbbed, the other man's snores began to saw through the swampy air.

Colin took the mound in the eighth inning with two men on, two out, and the team ahead by a single run. On the trot from the bullpen to the mound when he should have been focused only on getting out of the inning, his mind returned to the previous night's events. Flashes of Leyritz's mouth working on his dick dogged him; Colin began to stiffen in his cup during the worst possible time to get a hard-on.

Focus, he urged himself.

A ball-busting performance on the mound today would be a hell of an incentive for the big team to call him up to the majors—the stands were littered with scouts. It would also cement his value to his present clubhouse if he got them out of the jam.

Leyritz's mouth...

It had taken busting a second and then a third load to make his cock shrink enough for him to sleep. Colin had eventually drifted off and then awakened feeling more rested than he could recall. True, there had been some awkwardness in the morning, that feeling of having your balls grabbed hold of by an invisible hand once darkness gave way to light, and Leyritz had avoided making direct eye contact with him. Guilt, Colin supposed. But as the clock steadily ticked closer toward one more night at the motel in Buffalo, he found himself craving Leyritz's mouth. He had to have some more of it. He would.

Flashing his best game face, Colin fired a perfect strike across home plate and into the catcher's glove. The batter fouled a sinker after that—0 and 2.

Colin's thoughts again returned to Leyritz. His dick pushed against the prison of his cup.

Focus, dude!

Shaking off the catcher's signs, Colin settled on a fastball and blew it straight past the batter's swing. The ball struck the catcher's glove with a thunderclap, and known only to him, Colin ejaculated into his cup without so much as touching himself, squirting prompted by memories of the other man's face between his legs.

Leyritz *would* suck him off following the team's victory against Buffalo. Colin had a plan.

"I'm heading back to the room, pal," he said, excusing himself early from the bar. "I'm really beat."

Colin clapped Leyritz on the shoulders with both hands and bid good night to the cluster of teammates who'd gathered for beer and bullshitting.

Leyritz's eyes narrowed. "I'll be quiet, man."

"Don't sweat it. The way I feel after that game, I'm gonna sleep like the dead tonight."

Colin heard the motel room's door groan open less than an hour later. He put the next phase of his plan into action and started with the theatrical snoring. Through slitted eyes, he watched Leyritz creep to the other side of the room and strip down to his underwear, a pair of tightie-whities that glowed in the poor light filtering through the room's window.

The fake snores worked. Leyritz went fishing beneath the thin top sheet Colin had tossed over his crotch. Groping fingers invaded the trap he'd set between his legs, only to recoil suddenly.

Colin had gone to bed completely naked this time.

"Figured I'd make it easier for you tonight," he said, tossing the sheet aside to reveal the pulsating boner driving him crazy in anticipation.

"Dude?" Leyritz asked, staggering back against his bed.

"Don't worry, pal, it's cool. Get over here and suck on my dick, and maybe I'll return the favor...."

OPEN WIDE

Marina Saint

Okay, I know it might sound strange, but the best, fastest, and most delicious way to make me come is to shove a large, hard cock in my mouth. Or let me sink down to my knees, wrap my fist around it, and open my mouth wide before taking the head between my lips. Just thinking about it, just telling you about it now, makes my pussy so wet, it continues to amaze me. I like other things in my mouth, too: fingers, nipples, dildos; but it's a man's hard, hot dick, throbbing just for me, that puts me over the edge every time. It's not that I can't come in other ways; I can climax from sex or vibrators or even having my nipples played with. But my favorite way to get off is while giving a blow job, and the bigger the cock, the better.

The thing that gets me off the most is when I have to stretch and strain to get the whole thing between my lips, when I'm not quite sure if I'll be able to do it but every fiber of my being wants to rise to the challenge. Monster cocks, the kind you see in porn videos, make my jaw ache to be in front of them, to lick one and then the other, to have a gentle hand guiding my head, or a not-so-gentle one wrapped around my long, black hair, urging me on. Sometimes when I'm on the subway, I fantasize about being naked, my wrists bound behind my back, kneeling on the grimy floor, and going down on whichever guy is the hottest, while all the others watch. It makes me have to cross my legs, clamping them together and squeezing my cunt just right. Sometimes I get the impression the men I'm fantasizing about know exactly what I'm pondering as I gently lick my lips, shut my eyes, and let my imagination make me the cocksucking slut of my dreams.

Fortunately, I have a man to come home to every night who is more than happy to satisfy my blow job lust. When I met Kenny, my now-husband, I wasn't expecting all that much down there, to tell you the truth. You know what they say, big hands, and all. He's of average build, you might almost say petite, with only a few inches on my five-three frame, but I didn't mind. He wooed me with his eyes, his laugh, his fingers lightly stroking my arm and sending heat waves through my body. He wooed me by tracing those fingertips over my lips, staring intently into my eyes, making me want to melt into him. I would've stayed with him even if he had a two-inch cock, but luckily for me he's got two-plus-seven inches of meat I get the pleasure of dining on every day. I was thrilled to find out that what he lacks in height, he more than makes up for below the belt.

That first night, I went home and simply dreamed of surrendering to him, my fingers racing along my slit, then plunging inside, before I rolled over onto my stomach, pressed my favorite vibrator against my clit, and sucked on my fingers, wishing they were his dick, no matter what size. I got an inkling of his largeness the next night, when he moved my hand down to his cock while we sat in a darkened movie theater. Who knows what we were watching, I just remember he'd guided us all the way to the back of the theater. "That's for you," he'd whispered in my ear. I think he meant that he was hard because of me; or because of the tiny, clingy red knit dress I'd worn that night, the one that revealed more than ample cleavage and clung to my tiny ass, and maybe had given him a brief glimpse of my red thong.

But I took it to mean that his cock was literally for me to have and to hold at that very moment. "Good, because I didn't get any dessert," I whispered in his ear, already feeling myself creaming the tiny pair of underwear. I didn't think twice about sinking to my knees on the dirty floor and unzipping his jeans. It was all I could do not to moan aloud when his cock leapt out at me, without any underwear to restrict it. It was huge, definitely the biggest one I'd ever had the privilege of getting close to, and I wondered if I could handle it as I opened extra wide to encircle the head between my lips. I heard his soft moan, followed by a welcome explosion on-screen. I slipped a hand under the hem of my dress and stroked my pussy through the tiny thong while clutching the base of his cock in my other hand. My eyes were shut tight, afraid that if I opened them I'd see another set of eyes peering back at me. I can be somewhat of an exhibitionist, clearly, but at that moment I just wanted to focus on Kenny and his cock.

I savored the way it seemed to come alive in my mouth, my tongue exploring its ridges for the very first time as my fingers caressed my sex. I breathed gently through my nose as people yelled and screamed on the screen. Both his hands were touching me then, one stroking my hair, one squeezing the back of my neck. I wasn't sure if he knew just how turned on I was, but I wanted to show him with my mouth. I relaxed my throat and moved downward, swallowing even more of his shaft while shifting aside my thong to stroke my cunt. It was almost like he was touching me directly, his cock's essence traveling downward as I felt the head move toward the back of my throat. That sensation of fullness and power, tasting, smelling, touching his cock, is one I live for. I was so wet I figured he could probably smell me, and the thought made me slightly embarrassed and very aroused.

He tried to get me to stop, tugging me up and whispering, "You can stop if you want."

"What if I don't want to? What if what I want the most is to have you come in my mouth, come so hard I can barely contain it all, while I touch myself and get off at the same time?" I said as quietly as I could.

"Jesus, Cindy," he said, his voice full of awe as he then pushed my head back down and pushed his cock toward me. That small show of dominance, that act of taking control of this blow job, had me shoving two fingers deep into my hole. Not only was his cock the biggest I'd ever encountered, I was more turned on than I could ever remember being. When I chanced a peek at his face, Kenny had his eyes shut, a look of blissful ecstasy on his features, and when he did come in my mouth a few minutes later, I experienced the kind of excitement no other act, even fucking, can bring me. I had four fingers shoved deep inside me, and the orgasm that ripped through me had me shuddering for at least a minute while Kenny held me.

Since then, we've been inseparable, the two of us as a couple, and my mouth and his dick. I've blown him on highways across the country, in bathrooms, back alleys, on beaches, and in the woods. I've sucked his dick in every room of our house, and in countless positions. Sometimes I like to sixty-nine, but mostly I do it to feel how excited he gets when his tongue brushes my pussy lips, then plunges inside. We feed off each other, literally.

I've gotten used to the size of his rod, but I still have to stretch my lips to capture it, and every single time, without fail, my pussy jolts in response. Sometimes, he fucks me with a dildo that's just about the size of his dick while I suck him off, each of us battling to make the other come first. While I'm deep-throating him, he's got the sleek black phallus buried so far inside me I feel like I'll burst. Then he'll start on my clit, tapping it with his fingers lightly, then harder until he's basically spanking me there. I, in turn, fondle his balls, and sometimes wet my index finger and let it meander toward his anus. I'll do anything to feel that hot burst of cream in my mouth, that signal that I've given my true love the ultimate orgasm.

We each love to get the other off, and finding new and creative ways to do that is what keeps our marriage so lively. We also fuck, all the time, but those are often quickies pressed up against the wall of the shower, or feature me bent over the bed while he slams into me doggie-style. I love coming like that, too, but I always want to suck on his fingers, fulfill my oral fixation. Recently, Kenny got me a special sex toy: the Cone. It's a fairly large pink cone that has a motor in the center. I squat down over it and its vibrations make my cunt come alive. It feels like there's a rocket between my legs, about to propel me into space. To keep me grounded, Kenny stands over me and feeds me his cock, a position I love. Looking up at him, watching his cock enter and emerge from between my lips, is made even more exciting by this machine bringing me closer and closer to climax. "Open wide," he'll say to me, and I do, as wide as I can in every possible way—my lips, my legs, my heart—and he fucks my mouth while the toy fucks my cunt.

I know some of his friends (and mine) think it's a bit crazy, how turned on I get from oral sex. They don't seem to understand just how wet the mere sight of his penis makes me, how I practically drool with desire, how I want to kiss and lick and taste it every chance I get. And yes, I still check out other men on the train, still wonder what they've got hidden behind their jeans, but knowing that my mouth belongs to Kenny makes me smile in a different way, like I've got a secret and they'd be lucky if they ever found out what it was. The only man I want to open wide with, orgasm with, is Kenny, and together, we stretch ourselves physically and emotionally. When I swallow his cock, I'm not just giving him a blow job, not just making myself so wet I'm almost embarrassed. I'm telling him I love him, every inch, telling him I want him in every way, telling him I need to be that open if I'm going to be happy. I'm so happy to have a man who welcomes a woman who greets him every morning with a knowing smile before going about what she does best. I know the saying is really "An apple a day keeps the doctor away," but for grownups, I'd like to change that to "orgasm." One is rarely enough, for me or for him, but ours is the gift that keeps on giving. Even after I'm done, I can feel the outline of his cock against my jaw, the echo of my fingers or his or a toy against my inner walls, reminding me just how lucky I am, to get to be his full-time blow-job queen, and to get so many delicious orgasms in the process.

SKETCH OF A SUCK-OFF

Thomas S. Roche

It's dark when the footage opens; watching it, one might think at first that the lens cap's still on. But no, it's not that; it's just that no one bothered to turn on the light. The footage goes from black to that weird off-green color, revealing a fleshy, cottony landscape: man, woman, bed. The man and the woman are naked, and actually the bed's almost naked, too, the covers and topsheet having been twisted into writhing tangles and pushed halfway to the floor. The contour sheet's not looking so great, either; one corner's cringing under elastic tension and tucked up under the woman's ass.

"What do you know? The battery's still good."

"Does it work in the dark?"

"Hah! Shows what you know. It has impressive low-light sensitivity, marginally better than the EX-Three or the PP-Twelve, both of which have a much higher price point," she says. "I should know—I looked it up on Amazon."

"I thought you said you stole it," he says, scowling.

"I did," she replies, inching the camera closer. "I wanted to know how guilty to feel."

"How guilty?" he asks, his face now fish-eyed and weird-looking, mere inches from the camera.

"Pretty damn guilty," she says.

She gets too close, and he licks the camera.

"Hey!" she snaps, pulling the camera away. "Somebody paid good money for this stupid thing!" She wipes the lens with the sheet, leaving a wet smear illuminated in off-green. She points the camera at his dick, nestled soft and moist between his legs.

"Turn on the light, will you?"

"No," he says.

Her slim fingers appear in-frame, curve around his balls. She has longish, painted fingernails, but even in the low light the chips are evident—she's never been good at keeping a manicure.

"Pretty please?" she asks, caressing his cock, her voice like melted Scharffen Berger from before the Hershey's buyout.

"No," he says, audibly annoyed. "I'm camera shy."

"I'm not," she says, her fingers barely touching his cock as it swells. "Actually, I'm kind of an exhibitionist."

"I noticed," he says petulantly.

She turns the camera around, points it at her own face. Even in the weird green glow, a dispassionate viewer could see she's cute enough to light up the LCD, if your tastes run that direction—as his, pretty obviously, do.

The camera goes *Cloverfield* as she slides her face down to his crotch and pushes the camera into his hand. He accepts it, keeps it pointed on her as she lifts his half-hard cock with her hand. He steadies and focuses the camera on her face. In the green, her pale skin looks sickly, her full lips black, as if powdered and painted in anticipation of a night out at Mistress Decay's Underground Castle or the opening scene of *Studio Apartment Gothic Blow-Job Massacre*.

He holds the camera on her as she parts her lips and lets her tongue loll out, then wetly kisses his balls, which even a conservative viewer would imagine probably taste like her. She licks and sucks gently until he's all the way hard, which, contrary to his pleas of modesty, takes about a second and a half.

She trails her tongue halfway up to his cock and gazes up into the camera, smiling all wicked and wet.

"How do I look?" she asks, her voice breathy and thick and dirty and naughty.

He breathes hard.

"Green," he says.

"Tell the lighting guy," she sighs, and parts her thick lips around the shaft of his cock.

There's a moment of moaning while her perfect lips glide up and down, getting closer to the head with each stroke. Then she pauses, pulls back, and looks at him with eyes wide.

"WTF, dude? It's your first porno, do you want it in green?"

Off camera there's a crash and a thump and the camera goes bonkers as he struggles to save the lamp. He does, and the soft yellow glow suffuses her face, the shot going from green to golden as her mouth parts around his shaft, her hand cradling his hard cock while she slurps wetly up and down, leaving vivid red streaks.

"I wondered why you put lipstick on," he says, focusing on her. Her tongue swirls around his cockhead as she licks and lifts and drools a little; she emits little moans capped with breathy sounds as her eyes go from camera to cock and back again.

She caresses the underside of his cockhead with her thumb, keeping her lips an inch away, just close enough that her warm breath ruffles his pubic hair, and he instinctively strains to arch his back, lifting his cock to her. She pulls away and laughs.

She says, "Still camera shy?"

"Not so much," he murmurs.

"Good," she says. "You're about to become a star."

Her tongue comes out and seems to wrap deftly around the head of his cock, guiding it between her garishly red-painted lips; he moans as she slides her mouth down onto his cock, steadying it around the base with the slender fingers of her left hand. Her right hand caresses his balls, gently. Her eyes flutter closed and she slides his cock deeper into her mouth until it's halfway in. He can feel the head against the back of her throat; she clenches her lips tight and savors it, eyes closing tighter and tighter as if she's forgetting she's on camera; then she comes up again, leaving a visible red ring halfway down his shaft. She swirls her tongue around the head some more, then opens her eyes, takes a deep breath and looks into the camera as she slides him back into her mouth. It's obvious she has not, in fact, forgotten she's on camera—quite the contrary. She looks up into it as she pushes him into the back of her throat. "You little slut," he says with husky lust, "you little cocksucking slut."

Without taking him into her throat, she comes up for air, breathing a little hard as she rubs his cock all over and drools onto it, smearing her spittle all over.

Her words sound wet when she lingers over him with her tongue extended, looks up into the camera and says thickly, "Smile when you say that."

And a moment later, "He's smiling," she says, visibly pleased with herself, and she breathes deep and slurps her way down his cock, barely pausing as she swallows him into her throat, and the camera goes crazy as he loses his grip on it, loses his grip in general, actually, gasping and saying dirty words. When he finally points the camera back at her, she's down on his cock, all the way, faded pink lips circling the base of it and her cheeks smeared with the glistening remnants of cocksucker-red lipstick.

For a moment, she lets him watch that and say some more dirty words—filthier ones, actually, than she's heard from him before. She comes up gasping, her eyes glistening a little, a smile curving her face as his cock pops out from between the greedy O of her suckling mouth.

"You like it when I deep-throat you?" she asks, her voice notably changed by the intrusion. "You like it when I put your fucking cock down my fucking throat?"

"Doesn't everyone?" he says with some difficulty, zooming in close to her face, which looks only slightly less tomboyish with lipstick stains all over it.

She makes a kissing gesture. "Like I care?" she gloats, and slides his cock back into her mouth, all the way, taking him down, not as smoothly as the first time, but with even more evident hunger. She gropes after his belly, his chest, the fingers of her left hand fish-eyeing in the lens as she goes for his nipple, her right hand just clawing involuntarily and then spreading flat against his belly as if to feel more of his flesh against her. She comes up for air, breathes hard, slurps up and down his shaft three or four times like she's playing a harmonica riff, then caresses his balls gently with her tongue before sliding eagerly back up to his cock-head while she moans softly in rapture. The chest beneath the camera shudders and pitches with each stroke of her tongue.

"Tell me what you like best," she purrs, her tongue caressing his glans. "Tell me what you like the most about the way I suck your cock." She slurps audibly, her mouth against his glans as she closes her eyes to listen.

He's not in a verbal place; his small vocabulary of dirty words has mostly been exhausted, and he's gone visual, not multimedia.

He says, "Huh?" gruffly, and she likes to think it's not because he didn't hear her, but because she's completely blown his mind.

She brings her hand down from his nipple and cradles his cock, rubbing it against her red-stained and glistening face.

"I said," she coos insistently with a wet cockeyed smile, "tell me how to suck your fucking cock." In a lower voice, she says with a surreptitious timbre, "And call me a cocksucker while you're at it, there's something about that word…"

Overcome with pleasure, he's still not as verbal as she might like; "Cocksucker," he bleats, which turns out to be plenty for her. With a blissful moan, she goes back down on his cock, not deep-throating at all, just bobbing up and down, stroking the lower half of him while she makes love to the top. A moment later he finds his composure and groans, "Cocksucker, you fucking amazing fucking cocksucker," which seems to work pretty well, too. She opens her throat smoothly and swallows him till she's clenched around the base of his shaft, stretching her arms up and spreading her hands over his chest while she caresses him with her tongue, savoring the feel of his cock deep in her throat.

Then her precise instructions sink in, and he lets out a stream of shockingly specific obscenities describing first her innate nature and then the texture of her throat: "Your throat is so fucking tight on my cock and so fucking smooth—" which causes a little shudder to go through her naked body, a shudder he can feel all the way to his cock as the muscles of her throat contract around him, like she's swallowing.

She comes up for air with a gasp. She begins to lick up and down the top part of his shaft, suckling and caressing as he struggles not to come. She reads his body language and withdraws, looking up at him innocently, letting him cool down.

He breathes hard and she looks up at the camera, up at him, smiling, her face a succulent mess.

"Tell me what you like about it," she says.

"What?" he murmurs.

"My deep-throating. My cocksucking. Anything. Everything."

He gulps as she turns her attention back to his cock, back into harmonica mode. "The way you slide up and down the shaft," he says. "And rub it all over your face. It's dirty. It's fucking dirty. And your throat. When you deep-throat. It feels… it feels fucking good," he says. "It's fucking tight, and smooth, and…and when you swallow it it's like you're accepting—" but that sounds too touchy-feely, so he just says, "Whore!"

That does it. She brings her mouth up to the head, tips his cock at the right angle, and looks up at him, at the camera, as she slides his cock into her mouth, opens wide, swallows it. She circles the fingers of both hands around his balls, keeping his cock in position as she begins to work up and down in long, easy strokes. He says "Whore!" again, at which point her lips go around the base of his cock and stay there for a long lush moment while he moans.

Moments from climaxing, he growls, "Fucking hot little cocksucker!" with perhaps more convincing ardor than he's displayed up till now. The combination of words makes her grope after his crotch with her hand, as if trying to stuff his balls in her mouth, but even an inveterate cocksucker has a limit. She comes up gasping for air and coughing.

He asks if she's all right and she just coughs and cocks her mouth against his lower belly and opens her mouth around the head of his cock, wrapping her right hand around his shaft. Her words are wet, full, as she says, "Come in my mouth," coughs again, and begins to stroke him fervently.

He's being jerked off, not sucked, but the wet feeling of her mouth around his cockhead, her tongue sliding against the side of him, is what makes his eyes roll back in his head while her hand pushes him toward the edge. He makes a mental note to tell her exactly that, but it gets lost in the white-hot fire of pleasure exploding through him.

There's a second or two between his orgasm and the first stream hitting the back of her throat. She swallows eagerly, a hungry little moan coming out of her sounding wet. She continues to jerk him off as he spurts again, then again; as the spurts turn to drizzles, she puts her mouth on his head and begins to suck again, loving the feel of his last few moments of hardness, the taste of his come. She takes him all the way into her mouth, but it's easy this time. She keeps sucking for long, lush minutes, until he gasps and goes to push her off, then thinks better of it and lets her keep tormenting him.

She looks up at the camera and smiles. She lets his cock slip out of her mouth, dripping and glistening, streaked red-pink with spent lipstick. She rubs his soft cock over her face, which is sticky in places. Her hand is down between her legs, fervently stroking.

"Still camera shy?" she asks him hoarsely, hungrily.

"Not even a little bit."

She smiles wickedly, slides up his body as graceful as can be, and spirits the camera out of his hand. She relaxes into the ruined bed, spreading her legs and pointing the camera at his face.

"Good," she says breathlessly. "You're about to become a star."

When she reaches out to tangle her hand in his hair, he thinks she's going to kiss him; then she points the camera to her pussy, and guides his head down, so insistently that he can hardly say no, and after the first tug on his hair he doesn't want to. That makes him go hard again so fast that it's almost painful right after his recent orgasm.

A moment later, he's on camera again—and this time he's definitely not camera shy.

SCULPTED

Shanna Germain

Show me," I said. "Show me what you like."

My lover stood naked in the bedroom doorway. Dark eyes and dark hair. Such a contrast to his pale skin. His pale cock, too, surrounded by dark curls. Already hardening, lengthening, as he looked at me.

"Is that it?" he asked. "Is that me?"

My hand tightened around the silicone cock that rested in its harness below my waist. We'd made it with a mold kit a few days ago. It was an almost perfect replica—a little smaller than he was in real life, but heavier, too, from the silicone and the vibrator inside. Every vein reproduced, the smooth curves of his head, the way he curved just a little along the middle. This was the first time he'd seen it, and I could tell by his attention, by his eyes and his cock, that he liked the way it looked on me.

"Yes," I said. "It's you." I wanted to call it something besides *it*, to give it a name. I couldn't call it his cock, because it wasn't. And it wasn't really mine either.

"It's like a doppelganger," he said. "Seeing you naked, with your breasts and your hips and your...you know...and my cock."

The way he was looking at me was one of the things I loved about him. All that attention and assessment. He was an artist, a sculptor, and he paid attention. Not to mention that he knew how to use his hands.

Moving closer, he turned his head sideways, checking it out. He didn't sculpt real-world stuff—his stuff was abstracty, sexual in a way that I couldn't explain—but I could tell he was appreciating the detail. The likeness.

He touched the tip of it tentatively, as though he was afraid of it.

"It won't break," I said. "I tried it out while you were at the studio." A small shiver worked through me, remembering. How I'd pulled it from the mold. The way it smelled, nothing like him, but like us. It smelled like how aroused we'd been when we'd made it, keeping him hard so the material could gel around him. How we'd fucked after, him entering me with his cock, his fingers in my ass. The ways he'd promised to fuck me both places, to use his two cocks on me in any way I'd like. I wanted that, yes. But that was for later. Right now, I wanted something else entirely.

He was still touching the cock. His hands grew more bold, tracing the veins along the underside and feeling the place where it slid into the harness.

"You really used it?" he asked. "Did it feel like me?"

"Yes," I said. "Almost. Not as warm though."

"I bet not as big either. Right?" He laughed, and then wrapped one hand around the base of the silicone, the other around his own cock, as though testing the sizes. His cock was fully hard now, a long white arrow surrounded by dark curls.

"Of course not as big," I said. I didn't know how else to tell him about how it had felt. To fuck him without fucking him. To lie back on our bed and take his cock into my mouth—even though he was far away, at work in his studio. To suck it and lick it until it glistened with my saliva. And then to feel the tip of it part me, slide in. So familiar and yet so unknown. The way the skin of it felt too cool and rough, and how that had turned me on even more. So heavy inside me, moving in ways that weren't his at all, but mine.

I was so wet—just from thinking of earlier and from watching him touch it now. But that wasn't what I wanted. I'd seen him jerk off. I knew how he liked that. I wanted to know how he liked my mouth, my tongue. I wanted to know what drove him crazy when I was sucking him off or nibbling on his shaft.

He kept touching the cock, stroking it. "The detail's really good," he said. "Even the small veins...you can see them."

Artist, I thought. I should have known he'd want to critique it instead of suck it.

"Please, baby," I said. "Don't make me wait. Show me how you like it. I want to know."

He closed his eyes for a second, and I thought about what might be going through his head. I don't know that he'd even touched another man's cock, much less sucked one. And here he was, about to suck his own cock. About to give his very first blow job...to himself.

After a second, he opened his eyes and kissed me. My body strained toward him and our cocks clashed, dueled, in the space between us. Every time I shook the cock in my harness, it pressed into me, made me a little wetter. A little hotter.

"Please..." I whispered into his mouth.

He went down on his knees in front of me. Jesus, what a mind-blow. Seeing him on the rug, his lips near my—his—cock. It was almost more than I could take, and he hadn't even opened his mouth yet. I wanted to see him lick it and suck it. To learn what he liked best and what got him hot. All the times I'd had him in my mouth, and still I could only guess. If I ran my flat tongue across his head, he moaned. If I tightened my lips around the base of him, he jumped in my mouth.

But now, I could watch. Every movement of his lips. Every lick of tongue. Every suck and blow.

"Please, baby," I said. "Show me." My hips ached to push out toward his face, to find his lips with the tip and enter. But I held myself back, made myself wait. And watch.

His tongue first. Just the tip of it, pink against the pale silicone. He ran it around the head, wetting it, tasting it. The he kind of ducked underneath it and ran his tongue along the big vein there. He did it over and over, his flat tongue pressing hard, pushing the cock upward.

When he sucked the tip into his mouth, the cock pressed into me. Beneath the silicone, my clit loosened, melted. He left his mouth loose, not the suction or hard sucks that I'd expected, but more of a soft, wet slide. His lips moved over the head and down the body, making everything wet. His eyes were closed, and I could see him feeling everything inside his mouth, trying to figure out how it fit. He sucked it, slid it in and out of his mouth with loud slurps.

He took it all the way in, so that there was only an inch or so of the silicone visible. His pink lips around the pale dildo were so hot that I wanted to touch myself, to get myself off right there while he sucked. I was, like I'd started out, just wearing his cock, but as he'd sucked me off, it had become mine somehow, attached directly to my clit, feeling every bit of tongue and lip and spit. I almost felt like I could come with it even, pulse hot liquid into his throat.

I moved my hips in time to his mouth, loving the way the silicone slid in and out from his lips.

After a bit, he leaned back and looked at his handiwork. The silicone cock was shiny with his spit and almost as though it had grown harder, more erect while he'd sucked it.

He used his forefinger and thumb to circle the base of the cock. "If you had balls, I'd ring those, too," he said. "And push right here—" his finger slid back, between my legs, just in front of my asshole. My body tightened, wanted his finger there, too. Then he leaned down, beneath the cock, and licked me. His tongue tucked between my lips and licked from back to front.

"Oh, god..." I forced myself to keep my eyes open so I could see everything.

He didn't stop when he reached the cock, just kept going, trailing his tongue all the way up the underside to the head and then to the very tip, to the indent in the silicone from his own hole.

I was done learning. I wanted to get off, I wanted to fuck him, or come. Or both. I moved my hips, tried to push myself farther into his mouth. I couldn't help it.

He nipped the end of the silicone with his teeth, and then sucked deep and fast. The cock rammed against my clit, sending my head spinning. I had my hands in his hair, but he shook me off and leaned back on his heels, grinning.

"You wanted to see what it was like, right?" he said. "Well, that's it. That's the moment, right there."

"Fucker," I said. "You did that on purpose." My legs were shaking, and I realized I'd wrapped my hand back around the base of the cock as though that was going to hold me up.

"Yes," he said. "Fucker," he repeated, moving his hand back to the cock. "Do you think I could fuck you while you wear this?"

It seemed doable. "Sure," I said. "Why not? But first, I want that."

I pointed to his cock. Hard and high, it leaked precome against his belly. Now that I knew what he liked, I couldn't wait to get him in my mouth, to try out the new techniques he'd taught me with his tongue.

"Okay," he said. But then, quickly, he covered me again with his mouth. Sliding his lips all the way down. I realized simultaneously that I was thinking of the cock as "me" and that he was pulling one of my own tricks—get him thinking about something else and then suck him in suddenly.

I wondered if it had the same effect on him as it did on me. If so, I was going to do it more often. The cock rocked against my clit so that I was slippery and wet. Each time he went a little deeper and a little harder, and each time my clit beat back with a pulse of its own.

Wrapping his hand around the base, he sucked harder. With his other hand, he tucked a finger between my lips, filling me. All of my nerves came alive—even the ones in the cock, the ones that I knew weren't mine; I could feel them, firing, sending off small flares through my body. I came, long and hard, as long as his cock, as though it had to flow through every part of me to finally erupt.

I tried to pay attention to what he did when I came. That was one thing I'd never figured out—how much pressure and movement to use when he was coming—but I couldn't focus my eyes, I couldn't even see. *We'll have to do it again,* I thought, and then I didn't have any more thoughts.

After, I held on to his shoulders for support. "Oh, my god, babe."

"I agree," he said, not rising, instead looking closely at the replica of his cock. He put his finger on the tip again, sending an aftershock through me.

"I think it might be my best work yet," he said, his dark eyes raised to my face so I could see the play in them.

"Maybe." I pulled him up and then touched his real cock, the flesh and blood one that was a straight white arrow between his thighs. "But I'm not sure it compares to this."

After all I'd seen, I couldn't wait to taste him. As I went down on my knees, our cocks passed each other, bobbing happily. I put my tongue to the end of his cock and began to practice what he'd taught me.

AFTER DINNER MINT

Donna George Storey

I didn't give Ian the crème de menthe blow job because I felt I owed him sex for the fancy dinner or anything. Okay, so he did spend three hundred and fifty dollars on our date—I snuck a glance at the total when he was signing the check—but it was his choice to take me out to Chez Panisse. I'd have been happy with some good Thai food at a tenth of the price. No, I invited him back to my place because it was the sixth time we'd gone out, and he hadn't tried anything more than a good-night kiss, and he looked so tasty in the candlelight of the restaurant, it was all I could do not to dive under the table, yank down his well-tailored trousers, and give him a blow job right there.

Even after dessert—pear *tarte tatin* with cabernet sauce—I was still hungry.

"Would you like to come up for an after dinner drink?" I purred the words, arching an eyebrow vampishly, as he walked me to my door.

Ian hesitated. For a moment, I thought he might actually

refuse my invitation, but then he smiled warmly and said, "Sure, I'd like that very much."

Five minutes later, standing in my kitchen wiping the smudges off of my cordial glasses, I almost wished he *had* turned me down. I'd completely forgotten I'd used up all the Grand Marnier in my cranberry relish at Thanksgiving, and my stash of very quaffable ruby port had been demolished at an impromptu party with my friends last week. All I had in the way of booze to loosen Ian's virtue was a bottle of bargain-store crème de menthe I used for my grandmother's famous "man-trap" grasshopper pie.

Wincing, I thought of the collection of top-of-the-line single malt scotch and cognac I'd seen at Ian's house the night we met. He was one of the big supporters of the science museum where I helped develop environmental awareness programs for public schools, and he'd kindly hosted the holiday party for the volunteers. It had been a tasteful, catered affair with *tapas* and Spanish wines. Now I felt, well, ashamed. He'd just treated me to an exquisite meal, and I was going to try to seduce him with a weird green liquid consumed chiefly by drunks on the street.

Of course, I was still a bit tipsy myself, which is why it took me a little while to remember another use for crème de menthe, one particularly suited to my wicked intentions. Humming mischievously, I poured out two generous glasses of my love potion. Ian wasn't going to know what hit him.

I think he flinched, just a bit, when he saw what I was offering—the label proudly proclaimed the stuff was bottled in San Jose of all places—but he recovered his usual courtliness when I told him it was the key ingredient in my grandmother's heirloom dessert.

"The pie sounds delicious. I'd love to try it some day."

"Then I'll have to make it for you soon," I said with my best happy-hostess smile. "But I wish I had something better to offer.

All this crème de menthe is really good for is grasshopper pie. And blow jobs."

His eyes widened, and I wondered if I had indeed gone too far too fast. But then he laughed. "Is that another bit of wisdom passed down from grandma?"

"She was pretty wild in her youth. But actually I learned about the blow jobs from my master's thesis advisor last spring."

His eyebrows shot up again. He probably pictured something obscene, like me on my knees sucking off some gray-bearded guy in a tweed jacket. Which was fine with me, if it helped get him in the mood.

"She's a woman, by the way, and we got to be friends, so I still babysit for her now and then. One night I just happened to see a cookbook on her shelf, right next to Julia Child. *Recipes for an Amorous Evening* or something like that. Of course, I had to take a peek. Most of it was standard aphrodisiacs—oysters, chocolate. But at the end was a recipe for a very special after dinner mint."

"Intriguing," Ian said. His eyes twinkled.

"I haven't tried it yet, but I'm sure a worldly man of means like you has had thousands of crème de menthe blow jobs." In fact, he was nine years older and rather well off since Google bought his start-up—both cause for a fair bit of teasing from an underpaid, newly minted high school science teacher like me.

He shook his head. "Actually, I've never had the pleasure."

I almost offered to suck his sausage on the spot, but the effects of the wine were fading just enough that I remembered another bit of sage advice from my grandma: *If you lead a horse to water, and he won't take a drink, let the stupid bastard die of thirst.*

In other words, Ian was going to have to work for it.

As I watched him take a polite sip of the crème de menthe,

I tried to imagine him without that tie and crisp cotton shirt: naked, sweating, his genial face twisted in orgasmic release; below me or above me, the position didn't matter. I blinked. It might be quite a job to get Ian from perfect gentleman to rutting beast.

"Nice and minty, isn't it?" I said, licking my lips. I'd never drunk the stuff straight before, and it actually did make the inside of my mouth pleasantly tingly and warm. Discreetly, I sucked in a bit of air. A bracingly chilly breeze tickled my cheeks and palate.

The sensation was definitely intriguing.

Ian smiled, almost as if he knew what I'd secretly been doing and thinking. "Your professor's book has given me an idea for an experiment. I need a partner though."

I smiled back. My potion was working just as I'd hoped. "Experiments? They're my specialty."

He took another sip and leaned close. Instinctively I tilted my chin up. His lips touched mine softly at first. A perfect, silky tease of an appetizer. My mouth opened and I tasted him in the sinuous dance of our tongues—tiny explosions of warm mint with echoes of coffee and expensive wine.

I'd have to say his crème de menthe kiss experiment was a success, but we never actually stopped to discuss it. We kept on kissing, then kissed some more. Eventually, in his leisurely way, Ian had my blouse and bra off and was kissing my breasts, too. Or rather, he was savoring them, morsel by morsel, as he had the watercress soup with Dungeness crab earlier that evening. Now I was glad I was dating a gourmet. He really could do the most amazing things with his tongue. He treated my nipples as if they were the *pièce de résistance* at a Michelin three-star restaurant—sucking them slowly to stiff points, then lapping and nibbling until that hot, tingly feeling in my belly was almost ready to burst.

After what seemed like hours of teasing, his hand wandered lower, stroking my damp, throbbing pussy through my skirt.

"Jana, I want to taste you," he whispered.

Of course, I was dying to say yes, but unfortunately it was time to stop and have a serious talk. Ian had hinted he hadn't been involved with anyone in a while, and I'd had all the usual tests at my annual exam, so we were more or less good to go there. But I had to mention that the sexy recipe book warned you weren't supposed to use crème de menthe on clits and other soft, wet female parts.

Ian frowned and smacked his lips. "I can't really taste it anymore. But I wouldn't want it to be uncomfortable for you."

"Let me see." I leaned over and kissed him again. "It's still a little minty. But delicious."

"You're delicious." He cupped my breast and gave my nipple a pleasant little flick with his thumb. "I've been wanting to do this for a long time."

"Yeah? If you don't mind my asking, why did it take you so long to get around to it?"

He blushed and looked away. "I like you. I don't want to blow this."

I patted the obvious bulge in his pants and grinned. "But I want to blow this."

He laughed, but I saw in his eyes that old glimmer of caution mixed with something else. A touch of unfulfilled yearning? "Don't worry about me tonight, Jana. I want to give *you* pleasure."

Who could argue with that? But somehow I wanted to. That's when it hit me, why I'd always felt a strange, nameless hunger for *more* when I was with him. Ian had always been the one giving, first expensive meals and now oral sex. For once, I wanted to give something to him.

"Actually, Ian, it *will* give me pleasure. You already know what an adventurous eater I am. And there's nothing I like better than sucking big, long, hard things."

He tilted his head. "Do you really like it?"

From the way his voice lilted up, softly, I knew it was a genuine question. As if I had to be teasing or lying to say I liked getting cozy with one-eyed trouser snakes.

It was close to midnight, but the light was dawning big-time. I'd have put good money down that the ex-wife—Cathy I think her name was—wasn't keen on fellatio. Ian didn't talk much about his divorce, a good thing in that it meant he wasn't completely obsessed with the past. But he did have a faintly melancholy air about him. Now I understood his problem. The poor guy hadn't had a good blow job in years.

"Yes, in fact, I really do like it," I told him. "But maybe I should let you be the judge?"

I slipped to the carpet and positioned myself between his knees. I slid my hands along his thighs, up toward my final, glittering goal—his belt buckle. "May I?"

I guess he was no longer doubtful, because he breathed out a "Yes," and, always courteous, added a very nice "Please."

And that's how I finally got Ian out of his trousers. I'll admit, I felt a touch of shyness myself as I eased down his zipper. Of course, Mr. Dick wasn't a complete newcomer to the scene. He'd been hiding discreetly in Ian's pants on all of our dates, but this was our first official, face-to-face meeting. It had crossed my mind that Ian's reserve was due to some irregularity down there, but in fact his penis was a perfectly lovely specimen: a good length and very nice and thick. And like Ian, his manners were impeccable—he knew to stand up straight and tall in a lady's presence.

By way of introduction, I planted a kiss right below the single eye, then gave him a few soft licks right at the tender tip.

Mr. Dick twitched appreciatively. Above me, I heard Ian catch his breath.

I took the head in my mouth and sucked gently. Gripping the base with one hand, I did a little double-pumping action. His cock stiffened still further against my lips, and Ian arched into me with a sigh.

The truth was, blow jobs really did turn me on. Not in the clit-buzzing, thigh-trembling, road-to-a-rocketing-orgasm way cunnilingus could, but I felt a warm glow all over, and especially *down there*, when I sucked the cock of a guy I liked. Cock-sucking enthralled all my senses. I loved the look of hard-ons. They reminded me of some primitive work of art, a wooden carving, lovingly crafted by ancient hands. The thick, ropey veins fascinated me; more entrancing was the close-up view of the subtle crimson web embedded in the sensitive skin at the tip. I savored the musky smell of crotch mixed with hints of soap; the contrast of velvet skin and rigid shaft between my lips, filling my mouth completely, the way no other delicacy could. And I really got off on the sounds of playing the pink oboe: the moans, the musical sighs, the ragged breath.

But what I loved most of all were my lover's eyes watching me, two jewels glowing in the darkness. Yes, he was looking down at me, but somehow it seemed he was looking up, as if in thanks to heaven for a dream come true. Yet I never felt so real, so *seen*, as when I was between a man's thighs working my special magic with my lips and tongue.

Now I paused to look up at Ian. His eyes sparkled down at me like emeralds.

"Time for a little after dinner mint?" I addressed the question equally to Ian and his cock.

"Mmm," came the breathless answer from above. Mr. Dick, too, twitched his assent.

I picked up my liqueur glass and sipped about a spoonful of San Jose's finest mint cordial. Touching my lips to his cock, I dribbled the green liquid over the head like sauce over a sundae. A few glittering drops beaded in his pubic hair, reminding me of lights in a Christmas tree.

Next came the tricky part—I wasn't quite sure I remembered it right. I opened my mouth wide, so my lips didn't quite touch his cock and breathed out as I took him in about halfway.

He made a soft, strangled sound.

I paused, then sucked in air as I lifted up and off.

He gasped.

"Is it okay?"

"Yeah, at the end there, it was pretty intense." His eyes were hooded now and his mouth slack.

I tried it again.

He shook his head. "Not so much that time. But it feels good when you blow on it."

I smiled. We were already talking during sex, thanks to the crème de menthe, and good communication was a promising sign for even hotter things to come. I pursed my lips and blew on him, all over. He closed his eyes and threw his head back like a sailor tasting a fine sea breeze. I almost had to laugh—I'd given lots of blow jobs, but this was the first time I'd ever done much actual blowing.

I tried a little more crème de menthe, but Ian said the sensation wasn't the same as the first time, although it had a nice tingle. We tried balls à la menthe—again he felt a nice glow, but nothing special. By that time, I was no longer sorry my sofa was a cheap, faux-leather affair. Things were getting a little wet and sticky, and I didn't want to think about the stains our science project would have left on Ian's fancy designer couch.

As it was, the results of our experiment exceeded all expectations, but now it was time to show Ian my more basic, but no less effective, skills. I wrapped my hand around the base of his cock again and took him in my mouth. Moving slowly up and down over the shaft, I gradually increased the pressure and speed until his cock swelled noticeably. This was cruising speed. Sometimes I pumped with my hand, too. Sometimes I took him deeper into my throat, but I never let up. His breath was coming fast and his thighs tightened around me.

It wasn't long before I felt his hand on my shoulder. "Jana? Is it okay if I...?

I nodded, my lips still wrapped around him. Even in the throes of ecstasy, Ian remained the gentleman. To tell the truth, his sweetness was really growing on me.

I quickened my pace and sucked just a bit harder. We were in the zone, that fairy-tale land of pure sensation where the cock is as hard as rock, but the wetness of my mouth makes the flesh silky smooth against my swollen lips.

Suddenly, Ian grunted. His thighs clutched me like a vise and I felt the pulsing at the base of his shaft, knowing what would follow next—spurts of hot cream shooting down my throat. As I swallowed down the last drops, I tasted a faint prickle of sugared mint.

Still panting, Ian pulled me up into his arms and gave me a long and grateful kiss. I was happy, too—I'd gotten him as sweaty and disheveled as I ever could have hoped.

"Well, what's the verdict? Did it seem to you like I really enjoyed it?" I nestled against his warm shoulder. Already it seemed so natural.

"I'm convinced. But I'd bet I enjoyed it even more."

"I might allow you that," I said. It was easy to grant him one point, when I'd won all the others against such huge odds. My San Jose swill had done a better job of seduction than any fancy cognac. I'd cooked up the perfect finish to the perfect meal. And of course, I'd been spot-on about Ian's ailment—one good blow job and he looked happier than I'd ever seen him before.

My grandmother used to say: *The pot that's slow to boil, always simmers longer.* Three months later, I moved into Ian's place, with its stock of Highland and Island scotch and a wine refrigerator packed with Bordeaux from all the good years. Yet every once in a while we pull out my bottle of cheap crème de menthe for an after dinner treat. We both agree nothing tastes finer.

ABOUT THE AUTHORS

TISH ANDERSEN (a pseudonym for this shy erotica lover) was born in the South but now lives north of the Mason-Dixon line, in New York City's East Village/Lower East Side, to be precise. She spends the bulk of her time reading, writing, editing, taking pictures, and managing the subsequent—and dreaded—postproduction work. She's most comfortable behind a lens, focusing on the fabulous freaky folks that surround her. A fan of all things naughty, Tish is a kinky voyeur and a shameless romantic.

JACQUELINE APPLEBEE is a black British woman, who breaks down barriers with smut. Jacqueline's stories have appeared in *Iridescence: Sensuous Shades of Lesbian Erotica, Travelrotica for Lesbians Volume 2, Best Women's Erotica 2008,* and *Best Lesbian Erotica 2008.* She also has a paranormal novella, entitled "Fallen Soldiers," that includes sex with ghosts! Her website is at www.writing-in-shadows.co.uk.

ALESSIA BRIO is a sexy, sassy tart masquerading as a frumpy soccer mom. She writes poetry and erotic fiction, designs cover art, and edits the *Coming Together* charity anthologies (and she's won awards for each. Ms. Brio is also humble). Her fetishes include Sudoku, stainless steel, and rare steak. Alessia currently lives in the mountains near Pittsburgh with her three kids, two cats, and one ex-husband. Readers can find her online at alessiabrio.com.

TENILLE BROWN's erotica can be found in such anthologies as *Iridescence, Got a Minute, F Is for Fetish, Sex and Candy, J Is for Jealousy, Dirty Girls,* and *Rubber Sex.* She keeps various blogs on her website, www.tenillebrown.com and on her MySpace page, www.myspace.com/tenillebrown.

HEIDI CHAMPA has been writing for years but just recently decided to let other people read it. Her work has been published on Literotica.com and blushed at by friends. When she is not working her menial day job, or writing dirty stories, she keeps a blog, which you can find at angryinky.blogspot.com. She lives in Pennsylvania with her husband.

AMANDA EARL's sexually explicit fiction appears in Lies With Occasional Truth (www.lwot.net), *Front & Centre Magazine, He's on Top: Erotic Stories of Male Dominance and Female Submission, Iridescence: Lovely Shades of Lesbian Erotica, Cream: The Best of The Erotica Readers and Writers Association,* and *The Mammoth Book of Best New Erotica.* Amanda enjoys life with husband, friends, and lovers in Ottawa, Canada.

SCARLETT FRENCH's erotic fiction has appeared in *Lipstick on Her Collar, Best Women's Erotica 2008, Fantasy: Untrue*

Stories of Lesbian Passion, Best Women's Erotica 2007, Tales of Travelrotica for Lesbians, First-Timers: True Stories of Lesbian Awakening, Best Lesbian Erotica 2005, and *Va Va Voom.* Having procrastinated for long enough on her first novel, she has decided to instead write an erotic novel, in the hope of getting past chapter four. "Fellatio: A Love Story" is for MTS, her lover.

SHANNA GERMAIN loves to write about things that go bump in the night. Not surprisingly, her favorite genres are erotica and horror. You can read more of her award-winning writing in places like *Absinthe Literary Review, Best American Erotica 2007, Best Gay Romance 2008, Best Lesbian Erotica 2008, He's on Top,* and *Hide & Seek.* Visit her online at www.shannagermain.com.

T. HITMAN is the nom de porn of a writer who knows a thing or two about the world of sports—especially baseball, his favorite, a game that can get as sweaty and sexed up in nine innings as any adult video. He routinely contributes to a number of national magazines and fiction anthologies, and has authored several novels and nonfiction books, as well as the occasional script for television. His story "Long Relief" is very loosely based upon a tale he was once told by a painfully handsome jock who swung a mean bat both on and off the field, and who couldn't get enough oral sex.

TSAURAH LITZKY's erotica has appeared in over sixty publications, including eight times in *Best American Erotica.* Her erotic novella "The Motion of the Ocean" was published by Simon & Schuster as part of *Three the Hard Way,* a series of erotic novellas. Tsaurah teaches erotic writing at the New School. She believes it's never too late for love.

ROBERT PEREGRINE is a freelance web developer in New York City. Peregrine is originally from Birmingham, Alabama where he was a member of numerous psychedlic punk bands. He has had erotic stories and essays published on a few websites, but this is his first work to appear in print.

Originally from England, **TERRI PRAY** now lives in Iowa with her husband and their children. Her work, which ranges from the mild to the wild, can be found both in print and e-book formats from various publishers.

RADCLYFFE is the author of numerous lesbian novels and anthologies including the Lambda Literary Award winners *Erotic Interludes 2* and *Distant Shores, Silent Thunder.* She has selections in *A Is for Amour, H Is for Hardcore, L Is for Leather, Rubber Sex, Hide and Seek: Erotic Stories,* and *Best Lesbian Erotica 2006, 2007,* and *2008,* among others. She is also the president of Bold Strokes Books, an independent LGBT publishing company.

MICHELLE ROBINSON's erotic short story "Mi Destino" is included in the *New York Times* bestseller *Caramel Flava.* Michelle is also a contributing author to the anthology collections *Succulent: Chocolate Flava II, Asian Spice,* and *Missionary No More: Purple Panties 2.* She has recently completed work on four novels, *Color Me Grey, Pleasure Principle, Serial Typical,* and *You Created a Monster,* and is currently working on the screenplay adaptation of "Mi Destino." Michelle can be reached at robinson_201@hotmail.com.

THOMAS S. ROCHE is the author of hundreds of published erotic stories in many different subgenres, and a four-time contributor to the *Best American Erotica* series. He can be found at www.thomasroche.com. "Sketch of a Suck-off" was inspired by his disappointment on viewing the movie *Cloverfield*—great idea for a monster movie, but not nearly enough cocksucking. "Sketch" is intended as a companion to his story "Treatment for a Tongue Job" in *Tasting Her.*

MARINA SAINT likes to make messes, in the bedroom and out. Her smutty stories have also been published in *Naughty Spanking Stories from A to Z 2* and *Secret Slaves: Erotic Stories of Bondage.*

LORI SELKE lives in Oakland, California, with two men and three cats. Her fiction has appeared in *Fucking Daphne, 5 Minute Erotica,* and online at Strange Horizons. Her not-so-secret passions include home cooking, kinky sex, spoken word, and gardening.

Called by *San Francisco* magazine "our erotica king," **SIMON SHEPPARD** is the editor of the Lambda award-winning *Homosex: Sixty Years of Gay Erotica* and the author of *In Deep: Erotic Stories, Kinkorama: Dispatches From the Front Lines of Perversion, Sex Parties 101,* and *Hotter Than Hell and Other Stories.* His work also appears in well over two hundred anthologies, including many editions of *Best American Erotica* and *Best Gay Erotica.* He writes the syndicated column "Sex Talk," and hangs out at www.simonsheppard.com.

CRAIG J. SORENSEN's writing has been published in *Tasting Her: Oral Sex Stories* and on the websites Clean Sheets, Oysters & Chocolate, Lucrezia Magazine, and Ruthie's Club.

DONNA GEORGE STOREY's erotic fiction has appeared in many anthologies including *Yes, Sir; Dirty Girls; She's on Top; He's on Top; Best American Erotica 2006; Mammoth Book of Best New Erotica 4–7;* and *Best Women's Erotica 2005–2008.* Her novel, *Amorous Woman,* the story of an American woman's steamy love affair with Japan, was published by Orion in 2007. She currently writes a column "Cooking up a Storey," about delicious sex, well-crafted food, and mind-blowing writing, for the Erotica Readers and Writers Association. Read more of her work at www.DonnaGeorgeStorey.com.

Called a "trollop with a laptop" by the *East Bay Express* and a "literary siren" by Good Vibrations, **ALISON TYLER** is naughty and she knows it. Her sultry short stories have appeared in more than seventy-five anthologies including *Sweet Life, Sex at the Office,* and *Glamour Girls.* She is the author of more than twenty-five erotic novels, and the editor of more than forty-five explicit anthologies, including *A Is for Amour, G Is for Games,* and *D Is for Dress-Up* (all from Cleis). Please visit www.alison-tyler.com for more information.

KRISTINA WRIGHT is an award-winning author whose erotic fiction has appeared in over fifty print anthologies, including *Best Women's Erotica, The Mammoth Book of Best New Erotica,* and *Dirty Girls: Erotica for Women.* She is also a community college adjunct and holds a BA in English and an MA in humanities. For more information about Kristina, visit her website www.kristinawright.com.